BALLISTICS

AFTER SURVIVING THE Clapham Rail Crash in December 1988, Alex Keegan gave up business to write. Since then he has published five crime novels and more than 300 literary short stories and articles. He has won fifteen first prizes for fiction and poetry and twice placed second in the UK's prestigious Bridport Prize. Major publications include *Atlantic Monthly*, *Mississippi Review*, *The New Welsh Review* and *Archipelago*. Alex runs an on-line writing group, 'Boot Camp Keegan', as well as face to face courses from a chapel conversion in Llwyngwril, Wales.

ALEX KEEGAN
BALLISTICS

SALT

CAMBRIDGE

PUBLISHED BY SALT PUBLISHING
14a High Street, Fulbourn, Cambridge CB21 5DH United Kingdom

© Alex Keegan 2008

The right of Alex Keegan to be identified as the
author of this work has been asserted by him in accordance
with Section 77 of the Copyright, Designs and Patents Act 1988.

First published 2008

Printed and bound in the United Kingdom by the MPG Books Group

Typeset in Swift 11 / 14

ISBN 978 1 84471 477 3 hardback

Salt Publishing Ltd gratefully acknowledges
the financial assistance of Arts Council England

1 3 5 7 9 8 6 4 2

For Kieran Downes

CONTENTS

BALLISTICS

A SET OF CAR keys, fat as a grenade, is arching towards your eyeball. The tip of one key, v-shaped, will precisely pierce the dark core of your eye. You are not yet two years old but this won't protect you. You are not old enough to understand that these keys, thrown in anger, began their journey a year before you were born, that maybe, a psychiatrist will say, they began even further back when a mother left a father, or further back than this, when a mining foreman, bitter, too bad for drink, strapped his wayward son.

You don't yet know the word key, but you know car and you know picnic. This is where you are now, out in the soft English countryside, and the sun shines, and down there is a clear river and over there moo cows, and you have a mummy and a daddy. One day you will marry a much older man, a man with a criminal record for violence, who shaves his head brutishly short, who has his country's emblem tattooed on his chest, but nothing, nothing of this exists yet, not even this next moment, the long seconds when you look into the air, to the brightness. It's blue, and the black bird fills your view, and then something happens.

Your father might explain, if he could speak; he would be sorry; but if he knew this was going to happen, then he wouldn't have thrown the keys. If your mother had known, she wouldn't have insisted, she wouldn't have hissed *the keys!* at your father. You don't know *keys* but you know *car*, your car is big and gold and you've heard the rude words your daddy shouts sometimes, the anger between grown-ups. You don't know the word anger though, and you wouldn't say *fuck you* like daddy does now, and you would have no idea about letting mistakes pass by and you wouldn't understand a line of poetry, *she grinds my eyes with answers far too short.*

It's sunny. You're nearly two. You look up and the sky is blue and you are having a picnic and your mummy is taking you down to the river, but the car isn't locked and mummy and daddy are angry.

You look up; you don't know the science of ballistics, you don't know the word. By the time you will be old enough, you'll think it refers to guns and bullets, but here, correctly, it refers to objects moving through space, to initial velocities, height, direction, the exact, titrated amount of hate administered, momentum, friction of the air, the earth spinning.

You don't know yet about what happens to your father as he releases the keys, how his self-disgust spews out from him bare milliseconds ahead of realisation. You don't know, and he will never explain, how he knew something was *being done* here, not happening, that physics was a lie, that God was quantum mechanics, that there was no uncertainty involved.

One day, the week he will try to drown himself, he'll say, 'I could stand someone against a wall and throw keys at them and miss. I could try all day. That was *meant* to happen, *meant* to. I was fifty feet away, just pissed off with my wife. It was predestined. All I did was throw her the keys.'

You don't know what predestiny is. If you tried to say it you would lisp and amuse your parents. You look up, innocent.

One night, a long time from now, because your father failed to breathe in water once, couldn't make himself do it, on a moonlit night that to his family doesn't exist, you will be weepy, very drunk, and you'll say, 'How can you not remember?' and he will be confused and you will say, 'Mam had gone back home and when you drove us, you promised me you'd give me away, you'd take my arm, walk me down to the altar, give me away.'

And he, drunk, but not as drunk as you, will argue. He will make you so sad. He will only be arguing that he can't remember the incident, the drive in the car, but you will think he doesn't want to be your father. He forgets many things or puts the wrong things together. He's not sure why, but sometimes he worries for his sanity, he sees a bright blue day, his wife's hand raised to catch a set of car keys.

You will look up, see a child born thirty years before you.

Your mother will raise her hand. Her face will be a little red but it will not be in view. Her teeth will show because she will be muttering, cursing. Your mother will reach up to catch the keys. She will be angry. At the last moment she will pull her hand away. She has thought she might hurt herself, and has withdrawn. It's trivial, but you are behind her, in the shadow of your mother, under her protection. You are two, on a picnic.

Some time in the future, your future, you will be maybe thirteen, fourteen, already sexually active, already hurting, though you will think you're having fun. Your mother will be sitting at the kitchen table drinking oloroso sherry. She will be maudlin and she will talk, replaying the tape in her head. It was his fault —she means your father; it was hers—she should have caught the keys; it was just a terrible accident. It was both of their faults, because they'd learned to live on hate. It was God's fault. It just had to happen because too many things had been so good. You'll ask, 'But you and Dad split up?' and she'll say, 'Apart from that.'

3

Run ahead, see the day you get the first fitting of your glass eye. Your father has become quiet. He still works, still functions, but your accident has made him slower, deader. He is trying again but the woven bitternesses of your parents' lives will not unravel and he has learned merely to avoid things. He has taken to indulging you, to seeing only his 'Little Nelson'. He often allows people to persuade him it wasn't his fault, but he knows with the absolute certainty of death that it was his and his alone. He had tossed his bomb with the intention to hurt.

The hospital is the same one you were rushed to. Your mother and your father, your brother, accompany you. Your mother walks down a polished corridor with you, the floor is blue, the walls old and the smell will stay with you forever. Your mother talks about the magic that the lady doctor has done. She says they have copied your eye and when you leave here today you can have a special one, one you can put in and out.

The room where your mother takes you smells of alcohol, but you cannot think this. You merely think it's a smell you do not care for. The lady doctor seems nice. She has frizzy yellow hair and a red spot on her nose. She smells of peppermint and she talks gently. When you are sitting down in her special chair she opens a drawer full of eyes and then she says, 'Ready?'

You will be too young yet to understand cosmetic needs, but your mother and the doctors have told you stories about the eye fairy who is *far* cleverer than the tooth fairy. You tell the doctor yes, but after the doctor has cleaned your eye, suddenly you are frightened. Your mummy says 'shush, babe,' and holds your hand, then the lady goes, *squick squick* and there's a cold thing in your face. They show you a mirror.

When you leave the clinic, your mother holds back. She lets you run ahead towards your father and your brother. She has told you to run to daddy and you do. He is crying all over his face and can't stop. He kisses you, holds you up, then away from him, then hugs you, still crying, still stupid. Your brother asks which is the bad eye.

But you are too young for this, little one. You are too young to know that your mother and father have only one good photograph of you undamaged, that they will worry over it, have it copied when your father moves out. You are, of course, too young to know your father has been working away, that he has a place of his own but comes home weekends. You only know he likes to play with you but is more fun when it's just you and him or just you and him and your brother. You like the weekends, but in the week is all right too. You know this but don't understand this.

Look up, think of futures.

First the eye will be peculiar. They will sew a small marble into the flesh of the socket. They hope this way that the artificial eye will follow the movements of its healthy twin. But your too-young flesh will tear, your soft stitches will undo, there will be infections, they will have to give this up.

But you will have your eye. On photographs, sometimes one eye will be askew, adrift, and you will tell people, no, that's the good one, your seeing eye, distracted, forgetting to look ahead.

When you have colds, the socket will weep, a light yellow-white mucus will cover the inside of the lids, smear the glass pupil, the false iris. You will pass through a phase of embarrassment where to remove the eye and clean it is worse than having what looks like a disease.

Now for the next quarter second of your life you can see perfectly, but you aren't yet old enough to see what happens around you, only what happens to you and because of you. You will be six before you hear the word *Ruth*, eight before you understand who she was, and not until you are fifteen will you have the courage to ask your father was it her, did she cause all the anger, was she the hand that guided his?

His eyes will fill up. He will try to hold you but will feel awkward because you look and act like a woman now. 'No,' he will say, 'It was me, and me alone. Ruth was before you were born; your mother couldn't let it go.'

When you ask your father 'Did you love her, Dad?' and he says 'Do you mean Ruth?' all you will do is nod and at first he will nod. Then he will take a breath and tell you he loved her completely, absolutely, hopelessly. He will stand, go over to the window and look out. You will not be sure if he is crying but you will be old enough to wait for him to turn round. You glance at your reflection in a tiny mirror you carry and adjust your eye.

MIGUEL WHO CUTS DOWN TREES

WHEN I WAS A little boy, I had a wooden truck. One day the truck began to move by itself. It went around the yard and then it came back to me. I went to sleep. When I woke it was just a wooden truck.

When I was fourteen, I was flying a kite. I saw an angel alongside my kite. She was very beautiful. I found I could make the angel move by pulling the string of my kite, but then I fell asleep and when I woke my kite was broken and trampled with mud.

When I was fifteen, I loved another boy. He was beautiful, almost as beautiful as the angel on my string. My boy kissed me when it was dark, but then I was awake and my father sent me to a far island to be a fisherman.

I was sixteen and I was a fisherman who dived for pearls. But I was frightened because the sea has many devils. When another boy came who was very beautiful, I was happy for a time. Then the boat owner sent me away to work in a mill.

I was at the mill. A large angry man with a very black face, a belt with brass on it, hit me with a hammer because I smiled at him. He pushed me over some wood and took down my pants. I had to leave the mill and go North.

I picked corn. I picked apples. Sometimes women smiled at me and the men were angry. I bought a blanket. For a little while I had a dog. It died because someone kicked it and it did not want to eat. When the apple picking was finished I walked towards the brown hills.

There was no work in the hills. It was cold, even with my blanket. I met a man, not a beautiful one, but he was kind and he let me stay in his house. He had one bed and he made me warm, but then something happened and the man said I should go quickly. He gave me bread and cheese and a dollar. He told me the dollar would get me to the northern coast on a train. At the coast there would be jobs, he said. I could fish, for I was strong.

But the sea frightened me. When I got to the coast I did not ask for a job on a boat. I washed dishes where men played cards and drank wine. One day a man killed another man and then ran away. The police came and beat me. I said I did not kill the man. They beat me again.

When I was better I left the coast. I walked and a woman in a truck gave me a ride. I sat with her sheep. They smelled but they kept me warm and the truck went all the way to where the forest began. When I stepped down from the truck the woman —her eyes were brown and slow—she looked at me for a time, then she held her finger to her lips, and then touched mine. She left her finger on my face for a second, then she shook her head, got in the truck and drove away. I did not understand, but snow was coming so I went into the trees and built a shelter.

I ate a rabbit and a rat. I ate a bird. I ate some bread and one day the truck came and the woman came. She gave me bread and cheese and some wine. She gave me a cigarette and showed me how to light it. I did not like the cigarette. I took it from my mouth and held it. The woman smiled. She went away and I forgot the cigarette until it burned me.

8

One day men came. One man came and frightened me. I ran away from my shelter but other men were there too. They caught me. They pushed me to the ground and sat on me. They took me to the hospital in San Bartolomé.

After a while a man came to talk to me. He said my name. He said, 'How old are you, Miguel?' I told the man I was seventeen. He said, no, I was twenty. He said if I was a good boy I could meet the other people in the hospital. I said I would like that. I ate a pill and then another pill and then they took me to see the other people. They were people who walked very slowly, too slow to get to the trees before the snows.

There I met Maria.

Maria had long dark hair. She was very beautiful. I fell in love with her. She told me she liked me. She said inside her had been changed about when she came to the hospital. She said she would like us to be married one day.

The weather was good. In the days we walked from the hospital to the white wall and then back again. Sometimes we held hands. Sometimes, by the wall, Maria said to me, 'Miguel, the wall is not high. We could climb over it and run away.' I said that though the wall was not high, I did not want to run away. I did not know why I did not want to run away. I wanted to be in another place with Maria. Every day she kissed me and said we should get married. She said if we were married and we ran away a doctor might put her back together and we would have a son.

I was twenty-one or I was eighteen and I asked nurse if I could marry Maria. The nurse said he would find out.

The next day the nurse said, 'Maybe, but you cannot share a room. It is not permitted.' I said on the day we are married can we share a room and nurse said, 'You cannot share a room. It is not permitted.'

I spoke to Maria by the tree next to the wall. She was very happy. She said, 'We can marry, Miguel, and when you are ready we will run away and we will find a doctor who can make me a woman again and then we will have a baby boy.'

We were married on a hot sunny day. There was traffic stopped outside the walls and I could smell diesel and it made me think of the truck that took me to the forest.

I kissed Maria and some people clapped. We were not allowed to go to the church but the priest came to us like he did on Sundays and Holy Days.

That night I slept in the male ward. When I thought of Maria and got big, sometimes I saw Maria, but sometimes it was the truck lady with the brown eyes and a little bit I saw my angels. I lay down on my face and pressed against the mattress.

When Maria and I were married, I had one white pill and one yellow pill in the morning, and in the afternoon I had a pink pill and in the evening white.

Sometimes I was upset because I could not sleep with Maria or find a place to hide. So they gave me two white pills in the morning, the yellow pill and an orange pill. Our pills came in little round cardboard boxes and they were all together with our names on. I could read my name, but I knew my box anyway so it didn't matter. We all knew our box.

Sometimes Maria would ask me if I was ready to run away, but I did not want to run away. I was not happy and I wanted to sleep together with Maria, but I did not want to go over the little white wall where the road was.

Then a man called Pereq came to live with us. He was a tall

man with white, white long hair and sharp blue eyes like lights. He was from Brazil and he was a general.

He said look, and he told me his uniform. At first I did not see it. He said, 'Miguel, see? I have a bright green tunic, and here gold braid, and here are my medals. On my sleeve here I have the numbers twenty-nine and thirty-one. I have a silver dagger in a fine leather scabbard and I wear a pistol which I keep well oiled.'

I said, 'And do you have a green hat, with gold leaves on the front. It is soft and droops a little at the sides?'

'Yes, yes!' Pereq said. 'Now you know I am a general. Here take this red sash and wear it always.'

That evening I told Maria about my sash and she was unhappy. The next day, Maria walked with me past the tree and to the white wall. She said, 'I am unhappy, Miguel. I think you will never run away from hospital.'

I said, 'I am still gathering my strength. I will leave soon.'

'You will die here,' Maria said, and she did not kiss me.

That night, Pereq was very handsome in his uniform, and he showed me his well-oiled gun. When I held the gun up to the light and said it was a beauty, Pereq laughed and gave me another sash to wear.

But in the morning, nurse came to me. I took my white pills, the yellow pill and the orange pill, but they gave me one more pill which was blue. I said, 'Nurse, nurse, I have two white pills, a yellow pill and one that is orange. I have no need for another pill.' But nurse made me eat my pill and my legs felt heavy like trees. Then nurse said about Maria, how she was dead and the bed was full of blood and that a mirror had been stolen and was in her bed.

11

I was very sad. I wanted to be angry and though a little anger was in my belly, my belly was heavy and sticky and my anger could not jump out. I went to sleep, but I could not find Maria.

The next day and the next day and the next day I had my pills plus the blue pill. Then nurse said, 'Today no blue pill, Miguel. You have been a good boy.'

Pereq was kind and a good leader. So I asked him, 'Pereq, can I have a big fur coat, like a general? I have to travel a long way.'

Pereq said, 'Can you see my new medal? It is an Order of the State First Class and is encrusted with diamonds.'

'Of course I can see it.' I said, and Pereq gave me his finest coat.

The next day I climbed over the wall and I ran away. I ran a long way and once a man pointed. Another time children shouted. But no one came after me and I took some work-clothes from a hut and I ate some vegetables. I stole an axe.

One day I was walking along a road. It was straight like an arrow and was black with a line down the centre. A big truck came but did not stop. It made a roar and went by me and I hurt my hand.

But I kept walking. I walked towards snowy mountains and a place where trees covered everything. Though there was snow on the mountain, I did not think it would snow on me, so I walked as a steady man walks when it is many weeks since he has taken his white pills, the yellow pill, the orange pill. More big trucks passed and I became very hungry, but I cooked an animal that had died on the arrow road and there was water in the gutters which was fine but smelled of oil.

I walked this way until I reached the mountain forest. But I was a wiser man and I did not stop in the forest. I killed a bear with my axe and I cut out its heart and I sucked on it as I walked. I walked for exactly one hundred days, first until I could not hear the road, then until I could not see it. When I could no longer see the road or hear the road or remember it, I stopped and I built a house.

My house was wood. The trees were long and straight. At first I took some time to cut them but I became quicker. I built my house, and I moved in. I made a table and two chairs and I slept in a corner under my blanket. I grew a beard so I would look old. At night I sat outside my house and looked at the stars. I tried to remember Maria, but it made me sad. I had no sashes, no coat, no dog or a dish.

When I was thirty I went to a town. I told a man I had cut down a forest. He was amazed. 'Give me a horse and a cart,' I said, 'and I will give you half my forest and you will be rich.'

'Three-quarters,' the man said, 'and I will give you the horse, a cart, a leather coat, a plate and some gasoline.' He stopped. He held out his hand, 'And a woman for tonight.'

The woman was fat and her face was pink. Her lips were red. We went into a room and sat on a soft bed. She took off my boots. She pushed me down and I remembered a big man, a hammer. She undid my pants and was astride me where I had become big. 'I was married,' I said afterwards, and she smiled.

'I will have a child,' she said. 'In nearly a year.'

I have a radio now. I have a machine for cutting the trees. There is a road close by and the man sends a truck to me. He sends me boxes of wine and candles. He sends me gasoline. I have a refrigerator and a bed. I have plates and cups and saucers and I have pictures on my wall.

My house is under the greyest mountain. The mountain is steep and cold, but when the sun goes, before I hear the night come, the sky is red like my wine and I sit. I am not happy because I married Maria and we never shared a bed together. She broke a mirror and made the bed red with her blood because I would not run away.

I ran away, but Maria couldn't come. So we did not have a boy. I had to go to the town woman with a fat belly, big thighs and a red, red mouth. She did not kiss me. Maria kissed me and I loved her. The fat woman showed me a son but said she would not marry me.

Once in the forest I found a deer stuck in a tree. The tree was young. I could not move the deer, so I killed it. I left the head because it was stuck. The tree is grown now and has eaten the head. The branches have swallowed it. But I know where to look and I can see the teeth. Sometimes I drink by there and know a tree can bite.

I have a child, a boy and because I am old, I have an insurance policy. I will be very old and I will die soon, somewhere out in the forest. I will sit down, the snow will fall down on me and I will become the earth. And when the money is gone, I will be forgotten.

THE SMELL OF
ALMOND POLISH

BRIDIE COLLINS STEPS DOWN from the train, waits for the crowd to wrap her up. She looks above her: pigeons scattering under the great glass roof. Someone bumps her shoulder, rushes on. In the half-light she shivers, picks up her cardboard case and walks towards the ticket collector.

On the train from Wales, Bridie had listened to the clattering songs in the track. *Did she do right? Well, did she do right? What could she have done? What should she have done? Was it right, was it right, was it right?*

After twenty minutes, about an hour and a half ago, the train had slowed down, clacking and slapping as it crossed points, then easing into the dark Severn Tunnel. Bridie had felt her first real moment of guilt, then. How could she have left Pat, Jenny, Ronnie? And Barbara, Angela? Smoke had leaked in through an open window, but then the train emerged into light sunlight, bright, fresh English green, and she was excited. Now the rails whispered, *Of course it was right. Of course it was right. What else could you do, could you do, could you do? It was right. It was right. It was right.*

The ticket collector is a darkie. He smiles, has gold on one tooth. Bridie smiles back. Steam hisses somewhere, everything

15

smells of sulphur. People push round her. She picks up her little case and walks out of the station into a damp morning. She has nowhere in the world to go.

'I can give you nine shillings,' the pawnbroker says. He's bald and fat and wears a brown woollen cardigan, one of those funny little round hats. His eyes are red and watery. Bridie smiles at him, couldn't he make it ten bob?

'Two rings,' he says, 'nine and three-pence,' best he can do.

Bridie is at Trafalgar Square. She is leaning back to look up at Nelson when someone puts a paper cup in her hand. A pigeon settles on her head. She laughs. A man waves a camera at her.

'Oh, no thank you,' she says. The man takes the cup back.

She buys a newspaper, goes into a café to read it for jobs. The windows are steamed up. She borrows a pencil to mark the things she thinks she could do. The owner, one of those cockney chaps, makes a saucy remark which makes Bridie smile again when she goes for her second cuppa. When she feels warmer she asks the way to Bayswater. He says it's near Paddington, she should get the tube.

She looks at him. 'The underground,' he says.

She finds a public convenience and goes down. She washes her face and dries it with a towel from the case, then she carefully brushes her hair back with a little water. When she looks at the mirror she thinks her eyes look sad. She goes up, back into the day.

There are more jobs than people these days. Bridie can start tomorrow night. All she has to do, they tell her, is change any soiled beds and make sure all the old dears are all right. Bridie asks, would it be possible to start tonight? The matron, thin-lipped with a mole on her chin is surprised, but she says yes. Bridie leaves and goes for a walk.

The next day Bridie goes to see the Almoner in Paddington Hospital and gets a day job there as a ward orderly. She can start tomorrow. She goes to the pictures in the afternoon and falls asleep. An usherette wakes her. Is madam all right? Yes, I'm fine, Bridie says, just a bit tired. She'd been travelling.

That night Bridie changes some beds, makes sure the doors are locked, then dozes in a chair. She knows she'll wake up if anything happens.

In the morning she has a wash and brush-up, and goes to the hospital. They give her a grey uniform and a little white hat. Most of the time she seems to be bed-panning. The other orderlies are darkies, but they're very nice.

When Bridie has been at the hospital for four weeks, sister comes over and says, 'Mrs Collins, we were wondering if you'd like to be in charge of the other orderlies.' It's worth an extra five bob a week.

Bridie says yes. On her way to the old folks' home that night she has a vanilla slice with her cup of tea and buys another newspaper to look for a flat. It was a good night and she reckoned she got three hours' worth of sleep between doing her bits and pieces. She finds a bed-sit. It costs nearly as much as what she earns from working in the home, but it's worth it. Sunday nights they don't want her there, and it's still cold out.

Two weeks later, Bridie finds an evening job working in a delicatessen for a man called Stephano. She gives in her notice at the home. Some of the old ladies cry. The first night she uses her coat to cover the bed. The next day she borrows a red blanket from the hospital, sneaked out in a carrier bag. She buys a pillow case, and a clock for the mantlepiece in her flat.

Three months later, Mr Stephano asks Bridie, would she run his new shop in Tottenham Court Road? It would be days as well as the evenings, but she can have the little flat above rent-free. Bridie gives her notice at the hospital and the day she finishes, goes for a drink with her darkie friends. They all cry. Bridie buys an eiderdown and returns the red blanket.

In the Spring, Mr Stephano asks Bridie to come and look at a site with him; it's not the perfect position, maybe. They go in his car. Bridie sees a new office block being built two streets away, workmen clearing bomb damage opposite. She tells Mr Stephano the shop will be quiet for a year or so, but then it will make a packet. Mr Stephano buys the shop and gives Bridie a raise. Bridie buys a tablecloth and a candlestick for the flat.

In the summer, Bridie realises how slim she's getting. Mrs Stephano has let her have one of her dresses, but the other dresses, from before, they're all too big. She buys eight yards of Crimplene roll ends, and runs up three different outfits. She has her shoes repaired, polishes them, and buys more stockings. That weekend she goes to a play and buys a paperback book.

It's August when Bridie hears that Ronnie has passed his 11-plus exam. She sends a pound note and asks a friend to get it to him. The friend is uncomfortable using the telephone. She asks how's Bridie doing.

'Oh, making a go,' Bridie says.

About the time Ronnie is starting at Grammar School, Bridie takes all the furniture from her sitting room and stacks it in her bedroom. Then she pulls up the linoleum and sets to work with sandpaper. Every night, after finishing in the shop, she works for two hours rubbing down the boards. By Ronnie's half term holiday, the floor is immaculate. She stains it, and over the next few days soaks it with a dark brown polish, smelling of almonds. When it is dry she buffs it to glass, then lays a new rug in front of the fireplace. Next to the clock, above the fire, she puts a little china dog, a gift from Mrs Stefano. Behind the clock she puts her Building Society book.

At Christmas, Mr & Mrs Stefano hold a party to celebrate the opening of their fourth shop and the promotion of Bridie Collins to area manageress. Bridie comes in her new dress and wearing new shoes. Her long dark hair is brushed to gleam, tied back, falling loosely on her shoulders. She sits down opposite Mr Stefano's cousin, Maxim, and they talk all evening: about a wonderful new play by Arthur Miller, the new Graham Greene novel, the buildings going up all over the city. At the end of the evening, Max asks Mrs Collins if she might have dinner with him.

The next day, Bridie reclaims her rings from the pawnbroker. He seems much older than she remembered. When she pays he smiles and says they were worth only eight shillings, but he always knew she would come back. Bridie flutters her eyelashes and refingers the rings.

On the Saturday, Bridie goes to a new play with Maxim. Afterwards they dine at a small restaurant close to the river and later, take a taxi to Tottenham Court Road. Bridie says goodnight outside the shop and Max shakes her hand. When the taxi leaves, Bridie goes in to her rooms that smell of almonds, takes off her rings, and drinks a little gin.

On the Monday, Bridie rings her friend. Yes, her ten pounds had arrived, but there's bad news. Pat is sixteen now, unhappy. She's left home. They're going to take the children away from Tom and into care. Bridie puts down the phone.

On Wednesday, Bridie goes to Paddington station and buys a ticket. On Thursday she travels back to Wales. Maxim takes her to the station and for the first time she kisses him lightly, faintly, on his pink-shaved cheek. As the train clatters and December sun flashes, she remembers a trip in the other direction not so very long ago. When again she enters the tunnel under the sea, she takes a breath. As she leaves England, she dabs a handkerchief at the corner of her eye and sits up straight.

The train clanks across a dirty river and stops. Bridie disembarks, then walks from the station. Heads turn to watch her pass as she strides through town to the bus terminus. She takes a bus, walks from the stop to a red-brick terrace close to the canal, goes to a scuffed door and knocks.

Tom Jones opens the door. He does not speak. He looks down and sees Bridie has no suitcase. He's in working clothes, unshaved. He nods, goes into their front room, spreads newspaper on an armchair and sits down.

The house does not smell of almonds and it's dark inside. Above a dead fireplace the mantlepiece is cluttered with tea cups, a hairbrush, a drinking glass, papers, cigarette packs, ash, a silver mug, now brown, a school report. On the wall is an embossed plaque which says BLESS THIS HOUSE.

Bridie goes into the kitchen, finds two mugs, wipes them, makes hot, very sweet tea. Then she comes back into their front room and tells her husband they should take them upstairs.

In the bedroom Bridie undresses, climbs into a grey bed beside Tom. He is dark, urgent, desperate and silent, and it's quick. He smells of the steelworks she had almost forgotten, his fingernails are thick and cracked. She whispers to him. They drink their tea and she rolls on to her side. He makes himself her shape behind her and they doze until he grows for her again and it happens again. They sleep.

Ronnie, Barbara and Angela come home. Bridie is ready for them, in the kitchen wiping down when they come through the back door. She tells them their father is asleep upstairs and to be quiet. She dries her hands and they go into the front room. They sit on the sofa by the growing fire. She tells them she has to go back to London tomorrow to do some things, but she's coming back on the weekend.

'Do you mean it?' Ronnie says.

She looks straight at him.

'Yes,' she says.

'For good?'

'Yes,' she says.

In the morning, Tom comes in from work, makes a single cup of tea and sits down in the kitchen at a table with a check plastic cover. His wife comes in silently, makes another cup and sits opposite him. How was his night at work? He tells her there were problems with the rollers again. They'd worked all night in eighteen inches of water. Dai Evans got burned when a white-hot run of steel snaked.

Bridie makes Tom a piece of toast to take to bed.

On the way back to London, Bridie listens to the talking rails and hears the sound of her children. The Severn Tunnel passes by without a thought.

When she gets to Paddington she pops down to the underground, takes the Circle Line, changes once, leaves one stop before Tottenham Court Road. She walks down Oxford Street to see the lights. It's alive with people. Black taxis throb, stalled behind red buses, shops tinkle and ping.

The Stefanos beg Bridie to stay. Mrs Stefano cries and Mr Stefano offers her a partnership. They have been so kind, Bridie says, but they're making a go now and she's needed elsewhere. She'll finish the week and then go home.

She goes to work and telephones Max. At seven o'clock, she goes to her apartment, bathes in perfumed water, brushes her hair, dresses. Max arrives at eight, immaculate, in dinner dress beneath a charcoal overcoat. He wears a white silk scarf. They have tickets to Miller and they walk there, arm in arm against the night. Later they eat and later they make love to the smell of almonds. Max is kind and he whispers to her as they listen to London. They will have just two more nights.

She leaves her clock, her rug, her eiderdown, but she takes her books, the theatre programme, her clothes, her savings. She watches and listens as the train eases slowly out of Paddington. December sun glints on the lines but she hears no voices, only metal on metal, *clack, cah-lack, clack-clack, cah-lack.*

MOTHER, QUESTIONS

MOTHER, CAN I ASK you, with you and Dad, my father, how did it happen, how was it? Were you frightened, excited, was he strong, was he clumsy?

You told me once, before you died, you said, 'We walked out for almost a year and then, one day, on a bridge over the canal at *Alt-y-ryn*, he asked if he could kiss me.' You said you laughed, couldn't help it. He ran home.

So Mum, how did you get from there to being my mother? How did that shy young man learn to make love? Was he your first, Mum? Nellie said to me once, (she was drunk on gins), she said you had a beau everyone wanted, but he was 'a bit of a lad, a heart-breaker,' wouldn't take no for an answer.

I always wondered, wondered how I happened. I'm here, some kind of me, and I'm you, the bridge across the water, my hopeless father. Am I my sisters too, am I my brother? If they hadn't come before me, you would have been different, things would have been different, nothing, nothing would have happened exactly as it did. I wouldn't be this me, I wouldn't be able to ask these questions. How can it be that I exist without it being necessary that I exist? But how could these loves, bridges, kisses, how could they have all made my history, made me this, put me here?

You said once, you said Doug and Nellie were going to get married. You said you were on a tram going up Cambrian Road. You were opposite sides of the aisle and Dad shouted across at

23

you, 'We could make it a double wedding!' You told me that you laughed. You told me you said yes, but you didn't know why. Mum, you could have said no.

I remember you talking about the trams, the way they were always full, the way they clanged. You said they were big and solid and real. Your eyes were always alight when you talked like that, I loved that look, but it wasn't there when you talked about saying yes to Dad. On the day of the wedding, on the day of the wedding, you wanted to be anywhere on earth rather than St Mary's. You said that. Mum, how did it happen? How could you have let it happen?

My memories of you don't come in a line, Mum. They're like flashes of sunlight through trees, but I'm on a train going in circles, I'll maybe get to come round and see again. I have your photograph, the one from the war when you were in your ATS uniform and still had puppy fat, but I could see the woman in you, the deep heat men seek but can never understand.

It's black and white—well, brown, more like, and you and the other two girls, all that life-power, and yet the three of you look so soft, so quiet, just *waiting*. Did all women wait then, Mum? Did they just *contain*? I don't know how else to say it— you know I missed a lot of school—I don't always find the best word . . . But contain feels right . . . but I can look at your picture and see you with history waiting in your belly. I can look at that picture and I can see my life, all of it, see your grandchildren, your great-grandchild (Pat's Lorraine had a baby boy —pretty little thing), I can see everything, all the good things, everything.

Now you know what life is, Mum, was it all to come, was it preset, was it laid out, was it a book and we just flicked pages? Does he talk about it as if it was all so obvious, what else could have happened, does he, do they? What is it, Mum; I mean, what's there; I mean, do you now think it was all a landscape and we just felt our way forward, we weren't *doing* anything? Does that excuse the things we do, things you did, Dad did?

They probably knew about DNA when you were still alive, Mum, but we didn't talk about it. Now we do, we talk about it, about inevitabilities, about tendencies, predispositions. Some people say there's no free will, not really, even choosing or not choosing is wired into us. That's what I mean when I say contains, it's all in the belly, it was all there in your picture, you, and I guess my father, his father, your father, mothers and fathers, all the way back as far as we can imagine. Someone made my father; my father, he didn't. Someone made you, you didn't. You could have said no, but you didn't. That was wired in too, I guess.

I wish sometimes I could get at my DNA. That would be something, eh, Mam? I could go in there and tinker. I could give myself cancer or make myself big enough to fight. Imagine, I could have done that when I was ten, before you left us and ran away to London? Imagine if I'd been big and strong.

They tell me what happens, happens and it's not our fault, but that's how we are made, that makes a difference. It's whether we're built to withstand things or whether we are soft. I guess they'd say I was soft, but Mum, when you say something, people should believe what you say, not decide your DNA has some wrong bits, not decide to rush volts into you while you bite a piece of wood, make you eat pills until you're someone else.

I know you ended up here once, Mum. They said you had a nervous breakdown, didn't they? They said you lost your purse

25

and couldn't cope, that you started crying on the number three bus and they stopped the bus and rang for an ambulance. But you just rested here a bit, didn't you? Got away from the house for a while, from Dad. And I know what really happened to the money. I don't blame you, Mum. Dad used to bet on the horses.

They brought me here the first time when I was thirteen, Mum, thirteen. Now I'm forty-eight and how far have I got, just round and round on that train, looking for the light through the trees. I was here three years, meat, and they took away someone from inside me. When I looked in the mirror I was old, old as a child, Mum, grey and sick with sores round my mouth.

And it's all to do with you, Mum, my mother, and Dad, my father, and DNA, and fathers and mothers and monsters, way back to when there were caves and we made things out of stones. Mum, have you ever thought, all those deaths in childhood, diseases, wars, tribal sacrifices, fires, people falling into pits, and yet my father, his father, his father and fathers, fathers, fathers, not one died before he made a child. Here I am, forty-eight, a mother and a child and I connect to when we were worms. It's amazing, Mum.

Pictures are funny things, Mum. If you look at them they move, they swell up and then they go back again. People in the jungle say pictures contain the soul. Oh, I've said contain again. There's a picture contains your soul, your you, and your you contains everything, including me, and my little Jenny, she would be in a picture of me, in my belly, in our histories.

You would have liked Jenny, Mum. She's dark like you, has the Irish in her, the light. How, I'm not sure, but I think it's real enough. I read once that genes only pretend to divide themselves up, that sometimes they leap about in packs. If that's true I can understand it. Mum, sometimes I think my Jenny is you.

Here, when they go on at me, one of the things they talk about is circles, things going round, things repeating, me saying the same thing. Were they like that with you, Mum, or did they just know you were resting? They go on at me as if circles are bad things, as if me noticing the way things come back round is bad, but I don't see it, Mum, I really don't. We are mothers and daughters, that's a circle, and we're pictures, and we contain, don't we? You were a picture, I was a picture. Then Dad came along for you, and Ronnie, Pat, Barbara, me, we all happened, it's all circles; then I found myself a mother and back there again, round and round and round.

But why do they think I'm a liar, Mum? Why do they think way back then, when I was still just twelve, I was a liar, why now do they think I'm a liar? Did they think you were a liar when you said you'd lost your purse? Did it matter? You needed a break, so you started crying and wouldn't stop, and they pulled the bus over, called an ambulance, took you away for a rest. Nobody said, 'Stop crying, you liar! We don't believe you, pull yourself together!'

Mum, I guess you know now. I never lied.

I remember something. Bulmore Lido. I remember your fat shoulders covered in freckles, the easy blubbery way you swam.

I didn't want to go in the big pool but Dad laughed, grabbed me, and took me in. It was cold and there were leaves in the water, twigs. Someone had burst open a packet of crisps and they floated on the water. At first I held on the side of the pool. You were in a good mood, it was a sunny day, and you said something and swam away. That was when Dad pulled my hands from the edge and took me out into the middle. I cried and he said if I didn't shut up, he'd drown me. You swam back.

You said something and then Dad let me off. I went in the kids'
pool with the others.

You were such a good swimmer, Mum. I only ever remember
you as big and brown, solid and safe. You looked like a whale, a
ship, a raft. Like when you said the trams were huge and warm
for you, well that was how it was with me and you. Nothing is
solid now Mum, nothing has been big and safe, not since just
before I was thirteen.

I know you had to go Mum, you had to run away. I don't
know exactly why, but I do understand. I understood. Even then
I could feel things, know things, see circles of life. I knew you
were spiralling down, down and something had to happen. I
don't mean I could say that, then or that I can tell you now what
exactly I knew. But I knew.

When they go on at me here, they tell me this kind of knowing isn't a proper kind of knowing and that's why I'm here, but
it's easy for them, they have their trams, their fat mothers,
churches, mountains, they aren't like I am. They have to be here
to know. I don't mean just here, I mean here, where I am head-
wise, in my sad shoes—well, slippers, they won't allow shoes.
They were never thirteen, taken to the room, sent into blackness in a second. They never woke tasting wood and blood with
the world in a cupboard.

It was just before bonfire night when you suddenly weren't
there. One of the flashes is Barbara and me, coming down Gaer
Hill and she's telling me and I wouldn't believe her. Dad cut
himself shaving and hit Pat. We had burned toast with the black
scraped into the sink where dad's blood was.

Porridge and burned toast. We had porridge as well, Quaker
Oats. You did porridge usually, soaked the oats overnight, let
them get fat and soft. I remember fat and soft. You, I think of

fatness and softness and roundness and you big in the pool, swimming away, then coming back to rescue me with a light laugh.

When Dad was on six-till-twos, he'd do some overs, come back through the park at Mendalglief. We'd run down when we saw him coming. If they made a film of dad now they'd show him coming up through the trees (the monkey steps short-cut), dark with oil and steel, a dirty paperback under his arm. It would be sunny, there'd be Hovis music playing and we'd rush to him, he'd pick one of us up. His smell! He was darkness, tobacco, the steel, and some man-thing men don't smell of now. Pick me up, fly me, Dad.

On six-to-two.

On ten-to-sixes, the housenight was colder, echoey, but we just got used to it. Kids can get used to a lot, Mum, you would be surprised. They didn't take us away because Pat was old enough to do stuff and I was able to help with bits and pieces, but then she went too, off to London to be with you. But the ten-to-sixes were OK.

When Dad worked two-till-tens he never worked overs because he wanted to go up the Gaer Inn before they closed. He used to go to the Gaer, have a few Ansells before coming home. Sometimes he'd bring us all chips.

I think of you, Mum, when I think like this, I think of you, how you were big and brown, a house, a tree, a river, safety. I want to be with you, why can't they understand that?

GREEN GLASS

WHEN YOU SAY IT, finally say it, when you tell her you're leaving, when you finally realise that loving her isn't enough, not if she can bring you so much pain, your anger is so great you crush the wine glass you're holding. You watch as splinters embed in your hand, as a long, wicked shard of dark green glass hooks into the flesh of your thumb, your Mount of Venus, and you watch the blood from your palm, your arm, flow magically red to the floor.

The blood is everywhere, the rug, the drapes, but she laughs at your crucified hand, your slashed wrist. She says, 'My, honey, so much drama for such a pathetic little man. Rush yourself to the hospital, why don't you?'

There is a moment so black you want to kill her, then kill yourself, but you don't. You just leave. You leave her without another word, drive one-handed to the emergency room, get fixed. The nurse is older, thin-faced, with small grey eyes, a nose so sharp it looks dangerous. She doesn't much like you and when she speaks, spittle forms in the corner of her mouth. 'Hey," she says, "suicide, you need the stroke this way.' She thinks this is funny, '*Up* the arm, and it's better with a razor.'

You try to say it was an accident. 'Sure,' she says, and you think two bitches in one day, *Jesus*.

The first night is anger-easy. After Nurse Ratchett has sewn you up, you start driving. Earlier, you had thrown your typewriter, a bottle of Southern Comfort, a clean shirt in the trunk of the car. You check into the first motel you see as soon as darkness begins to drop across your eyes, you pay cash for the room, then you take the bottle, the shirt and the typewriter indoors. There are two surfaces in the room, a small writing table, and a chest of drawers by the bed. You put the booze on the chest, the typewriter on the table, strip naked, shower, then lie on the bed. The aircon makes a noise and where you're not quite dry is cold and tingles.

You lie there, look at choices. You use your thumb in your eyeline to measure each like an artist sizes architecture. Your arm aches and your hand throbs. You find that your thumb— this way—perfectly obscures your view of the typewriter, your little finger this way stops you seeing the bottle.

When you wake in the morning, your fist is bloody.

You leave and head West. With a cinematographer's imagination you see your rising dust trail. You smile faintly at the cliché. You don't play the radio, you just drive, drive. You can still see the unopened bottle in your motel room, the smears of blood on the sheets, the typed note, your credit cards cut in two and dumped in the bathroom. You're heading into the desert.

Three days later you hit a town called Boyle and some sign that says THIRSTY? THERE'S SWEET NOTHING AFTER BOYLE FOR A THOUSAND MILES . . .

There's a diner, a sun-bleached sprinkling of buildings, a gas-station, two tracks off at ninety degrees, heading into nowhere, farms. You stop, order coffee and orange juice. Behind the counter a big woman—her name-tag says Alice—with a little woman's eyes. She's dark-faced, old skin, but she's about thirty-five. She slaps coffee into a mug, and though you don't make eye-contact she says, 'You either killed a man, or someone's been killing you.'

You might have been pissed, but this doesn't happen.

'Thank you,' you say.

She smiles a big, fat-woman's smile, but you see the little-woman's eyes again; 'Well, shit, honey,' she says, 'you do look kinda bad.' The way she talks, you look a little harder. Maybe she's mixed blood, but no, she's just sun-burnt white. You tell her, 'I left without a razor.'

'No offence,' she says. She waits, her eyes soften. 'It's just you know when someone's carrying something, honey. Wanna eat?'

You don't answer so she says, 'I'll fix you eggs 'n' bacon.'

A year later you're still there. You work split shifts at the diner and in between break stones on her brother Cap's farm. You get three square meals, somewhere to sleep, a little peace.

You've put on thirty pounds. Now you don't look like a coke-head. Alice has lost forty. She started losing it a week after you arrived. Around this time, when you're crossing size-wise, Alice asks maybe the two of you, it's time you went to bed. It's like real but done light. You shake your head. You don't need sex, all it ever brought you was pain, but when you tell Alice this, something goes from her little-woman eyes and it's as real as a tree.

You know you've said something wrong. You reach out. You say, 'I'm sorry, Alice.' Your hand hurts. Alice asks you, will you lock up? She leaves.

You've been getting drunk once a week, with a sheriff's deputy from McCourt, a little guy called Ed. Blind drunk is usual, drunk enough to fall down and wake up hating. Ed is truly ugly, with a twisted eye and something not quite right with his lip. He's in love with Alice, but he knows once Alice wanted you and now she just isn't interested. This particular Friday you're rubbing the lump on your hand when Ed says, in his funny way, 'Things was all right before you come, Jack.'

You're sorry. You say it isn't your fault and Ed's twisted eye goes up, his other stares and he tells you he knows that. He says, if it was your fault he could kill you, but instead he's gotta get drunk with you.

'I'm sorry,' you say, 'I just stopped for coffee.'

About a year on, you're working out on Cap's farm when you feel a shooting pain in your hand and you drop the claw hammer you're using. Cap thinks you're sick.

You tell Cap no, you're OK. It's a hot day, white-skied. You say you think you jagged a nerve or something. This lump on your hand is bigger. You tell Cap if he doesn't need you tomorrow, you're thinking of driving into McCourt. Maybe you'll see Doc James

'Not tomorrow,' Cap says. 'Alice will be over, cook us up something good. We got company coming. Go Friday.'

You try to say you don't want this, but Cap speaks first. 'My sister,' he says, 'And you're as good as family, now. Angela is expecting to meet you.'

You thought there was just Alice and Cap. You tell Cap his sister never said.

'She wouldn't,' Cap says. 'They were identical twins, once, but then Alice started eatin' and Angela stopped. Then she went to New York.'

You pick up the hammer. 'What about the diner?'

'I knew you'd see sense,' Cap says, 'And Ed can look after the diner.'

One night, you and Ed aren't fully drunk yet and Ed says, 'I gotta ask Alice one more time—marry me, Alice. When she says no, I'll be going.'

You feel fuzzy. You finger the lump on your hand. 'Where?'

'Cousin o' mine across the state.'

You ask Ed is he sure? You tell him there's nothing going on between you and Alice.

'I know,' Ed says. 'I figured you were fixing sights on Angela.'

Angela is slight, her hair is short, a fine, light brown, not long and dark like Alice's, but the same eyes. Still, you tell Ed no.

At the wedding Ed looks fine and dandy in a tux. His black hair is slicked off his forehead and his permanent grin masks everything else. Alice is in white, her cheeks are pink and flushed. There's a baby due April, conceived on the floor of the diner at 02:25, she told you a little while back. Twenty minutes after closing, she said, on the edge of a cold desert night, after Ed had stayed behind, after he'd waited to ask his one last time.

Angela leans into you, she wants to whisper something. You smell her perfume. You know she's about ready to go back to New York and she won't be coming back. She takes your hand, and when she feels the lump, quietly she says. 'You should go see Doc James about it.'

You tell her you were going the day she arrived.

'That was eight months ago!'

'I know.'

'So why don't you go?'

You smile. You're worried about this, what's inside you.

'Jack,' she says, 'Go to McCourt.'

Doc James wants to talk. 'So, you're out at Boyle three years already and now you figure you need to see me. And all this time the lump's been there?'

You feel pretty damn stupid. You say so.

'You're scared of cancer?'

34

'I guess.'

'Then let me see.'

Doc James takes your rough hand in his soft, almost talcum hands. It's the first time someone has really touched you since you walked out on your wife. There could have been Alice, but it didn't happen. There could have been Alice's sister, but now she's going back to New York.

'These scars?' Doc says

'I broke a glass.'

'Hmmm?'

'Do you mean when?'

Doc James is still stroking your hand, all around the base of the lump. So you tell him. 'About three years ago. My marriage was a mess, I was a mess. I was a writer then, and she—'

The Doc cuts in like he isn't listening. 'Angela and Alice. Are you close? I mean, if this is cancer, would you want me to tell them?'

Somehow you knew. 'No.'

'Not close or don't tell them?' Doc asks and you tell him you haven't been interested, not since you left your wife. This is when Doc says he doesn't think you have—he means left your wife. He thinks she's still with you.

Of course you think it's a funny thing to say. Doc James hardly knows you. He's met you maybe half a dozen times, mostly in Boyle, just the once before in McCourt. But before you can speak he says, 'I'm going to have to open this up, you'll need an injection. Are you allergic to anything?'

The needle hurts a little, but only because you're scared. The scalpel is sharp but after the injection, you feel nothing. You're drifting, thinking of Ed and Alice driving to Vegas, thinking vaguely how Angela touched your hand at Alice's wedding. You can hear the doctor. You sense him pulling at your thumb, then he says, 'There she is, hooked right into you!'

Even through the Novocaine, you sense something harsh being pulled out from the flesh at the base of your thumb, a pressure gone. You hear a clatt of the scalpel then a tinkle of glass on stainless steel. You know it's green.

'Must have been with you since the day it happened,' Doc James says. 'Missed somehow. Then the body wraps it up, it turns into something slowly growing more solid.'

You're not really listening. You say something about being grateful, Doc. You're glad it's not cancer. You wonder where you might get a typewriter. You wonder if it's too late to stop Angela going back to New York.

L FOR LAURA; L FOR LOVE

A FOR ORSES, REMEMBER that? A for orses, B for mutton? C fer yerself, D fer payment? Not sure I could remember it all. I'm not even sure if that's right, A-B-C-D.

A is really for Alice, B for Billy Smith she ran off with. C is for Clown, me for not noticing. D is for Diane my second, after we had to wait all those years until I was officially deserted.

You know what I remember? It wasn't jealousy. It wasn't shock or shame or humiliation. As soon as Alice was gone I realised I'd never really loved her, anyway. No, what I remember was realising that the world was a lot shittier than it looks on Christmas cards (she went Christmas Eve). All of a sudden nothing was just simple any more, or innocent.

I know, for example, that Diane did it with Tommy from The Royal Oak one night when she got leathered on a girls' night out and slipped into his clutches. Trouble is, I can't make myself care enough to go round and give him a good smacking.

I know our Shell takes money from my trousers. I know she's secretly on the pill. I know that she got pregs one time and had it got rid of. None of this matters. What matters is it's secret.

Just like what matters with Perc is he won't just say, 'Dad, look I'm gay.' I'm not going to go to *him*. I could. I could just say, 'Perc, I saw you with that real mincer coming out of The Queen's Head. Everyone knows that's a gay pub. But see, Perc, I don't mind, I don't care. Whatever rocks your, you know.'

37

But I don't because *he should come to me*. It's important. It can't *always* be one way. It's not all me give, give, give, them take, take, take. There's got to be like a *quid pro quo*, things have to balance.

I feel like I'm something left on the side of a plate. Maybe I'm just too old, or jaded or something, or maybe I've just had all the goodness drained away. Tell you the truth I don't know and I don't much bloody care. What's the point of caring?

Caring always buggers you up.

Only thing in my life that matters these days is Laura. No, there's nothing going on, nothing's happened, but I like to talk to her, you know? It's been five or six years since someone laughed at one of my jokes or asked me a question about how I felt, or what I thought. I can't remember the last time someone other than Laura said, 'Hey, Len, it's good to see yer!'

Laura, she's what you call 'a woman of the night', a prozzie. It's really weird liking a prozzie like I do, and I don't mean like that, we've never like *done* anything, or even been in bed together. We're just good mates.

What happened was some bloke was giving her a hard time this night. I came round the corner and the lug has Laura by the throat. Well, I didn't think, I just lamped him on the side of the head. He turned round, big lad, murder in his eyes, and I thought, 'Oh, shite!' so I hit him really quick, as hard as I could and he went down.

Long story short, Laura was grateful and offered me a freebie. I said no thanks, but I'd walk her home an' that. We just got to be friends. Now if I see her I have like 'an appointment', go back with her, pay half price and we have a cup of tea and a chat.

Laura says there's no need to pay and she likes me coming round, but I pay 'cos I'm taking up her time when she could be earning.

Couple of weeks ago I told Laura about how Shell steals off me, and about Diane and the bloke from The Oak. She wasn't impressed. She said they didn't know how lucky they was and that they was really abusing me. I said, straight out honest, that I didn't care at all, didn't give a flying monkey's fuck if the truth be known. Now I'd met Laura, as long as I got to see her a few times a week, I could take any amount of crap at home.

But things are changing. First Laura started asking me to sit close on the sofa in her room, then to just hold her, put my arm round her shoulders while we watched a bit of telly. She says I'm cuddly.

Now Laura says she really would like her and me to do it, you know, go to bed together. She says she'd even take a day off so she wasn't seeing anyone on business and we could be together all day, just like a couple, maybe have breakfast, go shopping, come back, snuggle up in bed, then actually do it. She says, though, that this day I wouldn't pay, 'cos it's not like that. This would be because she wants *me*, it's not business. She'd kiss me and that. She never kisses clients.

I thought about it. It's not that I don't find Laura attractive. Bloody hell, it's the opposite! But if it happens between me and Laura then I want it all out in the open, above board. I don't want to cheat or anything.

So we're saving, me and Laura. I give her sixty quid a week which she's putting away for us. In a year's time we'll have £3,000. Then I'll empty my Post Office account, put the £7,000 with the three and we'll be off.

Laura will look after the ten grand while I go round to tell Diane. Just because none of them have ever been straight with me, doesn't mean I can't do the right thing.

I'll tell Diane, she can go with the guy from The Oak if she wants, but I'm going away.

Then I'll go back to Laura's place and she'll be waiting.

AN OLD MAN WATCHING FOOTBALL AFTER SUNDAY LUNCH

I'M AN OLD MAN watching football after Sunday lunch. Earlier we went to The Sun in the Wood. I had Cold Turkey, Mary had Roast Lamb, her mother looked like mutton dressed up, with mint sauce. There we were, lording it, our Sunday best, our table reserved as usual in the annexe, four bottles of Chateau Neuf du Pape opened and breathing, waiting for us when we arrived. El Perfecto!

My grandson plays soccer. (The manager is a clown.) It's a crap day, wet, wind, and I have to remind myself I'm here to watch my boy. When he pulls on that red shirt I realise he is the most important thing to me.

Let me backtrack a moment. For my pains, years back, I sold my one decent novel. Now I hack out lousy copies, shadows of that first one, and for whatever reason I still get booked to talk to writers. Yesterday I was in Wales, a shit-hole seaside resort called Porthcawl—a writers conference—and I found myself visiting the town's Rest Bay Hotel, a hotel for gentlefolks.

Before I travelled, in the morning I'm out on the drive. It's dark, raining, I'm loading the car, I get this damn nosebleed, fucking thing. Spot. Spot. Blood in the back of the car. This is all I need.

I've already trundled a case full of books to the car and raised a sweat humping it over the tailgate and into the back.

I'm thinking, 'Boy, You Got to Carry That Weight' and trying to remember the song, but it moves away, I'm just a sad old fuck with long white hair, one good book, and a runny, bloody nose.

My grandkid, his name is Peter. Last Christmas he gave me an Apple iPod. (Well, I know it's from my son, but it was Peter who gave me the box.) I may be old, but I'm not one of those olds who can't embrace the new technologies.

I have this trick I've perfected. When I drive I always go real early in the morning. I plug the iPod into the cigar lighter, ear-up and shut out the world. If you travel early, eared-up like this, the world is a black tube, and after ten, fifteen minutes of motorway you can enter a zen-like state.

Is it dangerous? Oh, I hope it's lethal, but the point is you can cross a country (and get to a conference) without once thinking about it. And if you have had my life, non-thinking is a good thing.

Peter hasn't been picked to start, but he's substitute, jigging up and down on the line, tiny mud splatters appearing on his white socks.

When I got to Porthcawl, I was early. I climbed stiffly from the car, unbent my metal knee, pulled the case full of books from the boot and trundled inside through the drizzle. Old ladies, residents, stared at me.

There's nobody to greet me, the honoured guest. I'm an hour too early for being an hour early. I go into a common room. It smells faintly of damp and aerosolled-away human waste, a sad smell. On tables I see Scrabble, chess sets, large-print books, and I have this wave roll through me, revulsion for the old (of which I am one).

I'm thinking, Death, anytime you like, but be swift and true, my friend. Two women zimmer past and I think, do it any way you damn like, as long as I don't end up in Porthcawl.

The game is ten minutes old and we are 2-0 down. Our tactics are terrible, the wings are starved of ball, so effectively we are playing with nine men. Peter is cursing and shaking his head, desperate to get on and make his mark. I'm thinking, Peter you're playing in the wrong position in the wrong team for the wrong damn manager, and fifty years too late. (I was a good midfielder and I would have fed Peter through balls, kept running, got the return pass and buried the ball in the net.)

The talk? Oh, it went fine. I introduced myself and watched the awe move through the room, then I cracked a standard joke about my long white hair, then I asked who in the room wanted to write and who there wanted to be a writer?

We chatted (that's almost all my talks are these days) and then I read a chapter from *The Stars Beneath Their Feet*. Someone in the back of the room began to quietly weep.

But now I am looking at this shambles of a football game, aware of Peter jogging beside me, but something happens, gives way, and I remember (not facts, movement or incident, but remember with my blood, feel things in my balls). I remember the trip to Wales.

Smells connect to the soul. Music does too. I have the iPod set to random play, but today God, bored again, set the playlist to 'fuck'.

Song one and two I don't remember. Three is 'A Groovy Kind of Love' and I remember Kathy. I sail past a lorry so big it pulls a trailer and the food it carries could probably maintain a city for a week. Ah, Kathy!

You ever wonder how red becomes grey, how alive becomes

surviving? You ever see film star X and starlet Y and read about their break-ups, their new passions and think *I wish*? You ever flip that wish and wonder about the underside? Where there is love there is always pain, the stars are not only above us.

Oh, I let Kathy go, sweet, simple Kathy. Sweet Kathy who was only pretty, only sweet. Kathy who loved this guy who was pretty damn good on the ball, wrote little poems, dreamed of writing a novel. Groovy Kind of Love.

My kids (Peter's father and his uncle Tom)—they tootle. My kids they cruise, they coast, they float. My kids blob along on a crazy, slow, lazy river. When the river reaches the falls they'll be asleep.

But Peter out there, my kid's kid, in his little chest beats a little heart and his muscles course with possibility, but already he's learned to jog on the sidelines and wait his turn, because some jackass with a soft belly has the title Manager.

This song sequence yesterday morning, I think it was a message. My damn nose started bleeding again, and the songs just came at me, in waves, attack after attack, crooners sneering, all the bad things I'd done, the places I despised, the women I had discarded.

I was passing Swindon when I started to cry. I managed to hold on to each sin, each piled-up, dumb, tin-pan-alley trick-emotion; but, like the smell of love, like Kathy's ear-dabbed Tweed, like the dull odour of my father's death, nothing went away. It accumulated.

And I remembered that I was old, I was a fraud. I knew I acted for middle-aged writing teachers who were gleefully surprised I came so cheap, the author of the dazzling *Stars Beneath Their Feet*. I remembered how much of a shit I was, how I had hurt people, and then I remembered how I let my other wives persuade me that leaving a woman was never anything to do with weakness, or a fault in me. No, they weren't enough. Then the writer of *Stars Beneath* needed what the writer of *Stars Beneath* was now about to receive, this dark woman, this weight, these spread legs, this sacrificial sucking.

And I wept, slowly, as the sun rose, as I swept up and over the verdigris V of the Severn Bridge, and onwards, always falling, to Porthcawl.

Yesterday I read something: a short story, that's all. 'The Girl in the Flammable Skirt'. I didn't understand it. I wasn't meant to, yet it ached. It ached with what was once in my bowels, my heart, and my stupid, desperate prick. It ached with whatever it was made me cry when I came into Kathy. It ached with whatever it was that lined up these songs and made me cry from Swindon to Cardiff in my black tube, in my silences, swishing at seventy, downhill.

And here I am now, old, empty, fraudulent. I could eat this fucking manager, eat him up and spit him out and not break step. This moron who finally has allowed Peter his chance on the pitch.

But as I watch, the ball never comes near, never comes near, and little Peter, who flies like the wind, can fly like the wind, his head drops, and I hear this moronic manager mutter to his left. I hear my surname and I know he's not worth shit.

This is when I disgrace myself. I take off my old writer's warm grey coat and run on to the pitch. There is a lump with the ball. I hit him hard and come away, leather close to my feet.

'Peter!' I shout, and I push a through ball ten yards in front of him. He barely hesitates. He runs it down, cuts inside one defender and outside another. He must hear me shout, 'Near Post!' and the ball comes over, gold against the sky.

I haven't stopped and the ball, falling, is there, almost. I have to dive to connect, and I do, gloriously, the ball leaving thick, dark mud on my forehead and in my white hair as it *slams* into the net and I slam into the ground. I hear the referee's whistle.

A man has run on the pitch. Some silly old codger, clattered some lad. Crazy old bastard.

I get up and like I am iPodded in my slithering car, I hear but hear-not the blathering idiots, the lifeless, sexless floating things. I'm kneeling now, barely breathing. Something is coming out of my nose. When I say, *what d'you think of that pass, then, Petesy?* it comes out blubbery and suddenly I wonder if I'm dying.

Now I look at Petesy and there's the light that wasn't in my son, but is in him. He's laughing. He's telling me there isn't a granddad on the *planet* who could do what we just did. He says was that a sweet cross or what, gramps? and I say, never mind the bloody cross, what about my diving header?

Now I'm wondering as this blood continues, but I think, *Death? Could you just give me a minute?*

I'm actually negotiating, figuring I need five minutes here, then at least five more years. So I block one half of my nose and blow, block the other side, blow. I get up.

The fishmouths are still going, but I am in my tube. I tell them Peter has just resigned, and I grab his hand and we walk away. I'm thinking about iPods, tunnels, *The Stars Beneath My Feet*, and sequels. I am covered in mud.

THE FUCKING POINT TWO

MY BROTHER'S HABIT IS bloody annoying. He's Friar Tuck and I'm running as Maid Marion and we are only four miles into the London Marathon and the swish-swish-swish-fucking-swish is driving me crazy.

'Fer Christ's sake, Colin, I *told* you. Go as the Fucking Sheriff of Fucking Nottingham. We'll never catch Robin Hood and Little John now and that's me and you down fifty fucking quid each.'

'Ah, fuck off, *brother*,' Colin says (he always says it like that, *brother*, heavy on the emphasis). Then he reminds me this is his seventeenth marathon and Robin and Little John have gone off far too fast.

Don't ask me why we do it, raise this money. Don't ask me, because I know and telling people breaks my heart, but why do we dress like total fucking idiots every time? My forty-seven-inch D-cups make Jordan look anorexic but fucking *hell* do they bounce, swish-swish-fucking-swish and bounce-bounce-bounce, *and we have twenty-two miles to go.*

'Twenty-two point two,' Colin reminds me, swish-swish, bounce-bounce. 'Never forget the point two. The number of people who think twenty-six and end up on their arses, three hundred yards to go . . .'

I need to get into the zone, settle into the rhythm. Running a marathon is as much in the head as in the heart and lungs. You have to settle down, not get too excited (twenty-six point two

47

miles is a long way), run within yourself, and if you've trained properly, just remember you run twenty miles and then you have to run another six point two. Never forget the point two.

The rebels had an odd badge, a blue apple. After they cleansed a village, they would paint their damn blue apples everywhere. White squares, blue apples, and so much blood.

They liked to finish people off with machetes.

I'm thirty-two. Thirty-two, fit. I run marathons. Colin and I climb, we white-water raft, we fly hang-gliders, we surf off Newquay. We do lots of things. Things that are easy with two legs. Easy with legs with feet on the end. We are young men, but sometimes, especially last thing at night, or passing a glossy display of red and green apples in the supermarket, I feel old, old, old. And empty.

I was in the mob, a sprog, a foot-soldier, a para, feels like almost before I was shaving, then I came under fire, the real thing and forgive me, but I loved it. I loved the way the world came down to just you, your mates, staying alive. I loved it so much I trained twice as hard, even tried for the SAS. It's not Hollywood, not ever, but even losing buddies you get used to. That's why, when I came out I straight away signed up to go to Africa. I hadn't had enough.

We are passing the ten mile marker. Colin's saying something. Apparently one of my tits has shifted position. I shove it down. The crowd laughs and someone starts a chant, 'Get-yer tits out for the boys!'

We'd stopped singing three months into that dirty war. We'd

stopped most things. I kept a diary back then—we all had visions of being Andy McNab—and reading it now, what strikes me still is how we avoided our feelings. We saw the world as them, the fucking rebels. The rebels did this, fucking disgusting; the rebels did that, fucking evil; we walked in on this, fucking unbelievable.

Thirty, we're gonna live for fucking ever. What we didn't do was think. What you don't ever do is think. Thinking can slow you down and there's sometimes a split-second difference between killing and killed. We just did our job.

Thirteen miles. No, it's not halfway. Don't forget the point two. Colin is like a metronome now. I would be if it wasn't for these tits. We go along easily, eight-minute miling. We've run together like this with packs on, carrying weapons, and we both ran sub-three-hour marathons before we started raising money for the charity and had to dress up.

'Oi, Marion, fancy a shag?'

'Oi, Tuck! Ooo ate all the pies?'

We wave back, grin. Suddenly for no reason at all I imagine blowing the two blokes away, the women nearby going down too, collateral damage. Instead I shove my tits up and wave.

I know the day when I decided enough was enough. We were clearing a town about ten miles from the capital. The Blue Apples had been there, swept in, swept out. We knew there'd be bodies, but even hard bastards like us weren't ready for what we found that day. Carnage.

We went in before sunrise, laid under cover and obboed the place for movement. Nothing. Me, Colin, half a dozen others, Robin Hood and Little John, got up and walked in. The other half of the squad watched our backs.

49

Seventeen miles. About four hundred yards ahead I think I can make out Robin and John from the way they are running.

We walk in, careful, alert, but we just know there's nothing alive. That's when we see the cat. Bits of it are trailing behind it, and it's making this sound that'd break your heart. Colin stamped on its head and the noise stopped. Then we came across a used-car lot, all the windows of the cars broken, the back seat of one of them crawling with those little brown stinging caterpillars.

Nineteen miles. Definitely them three hundred ahead.

We heard a window or a door clatter. When we got up, nothing. In one house, what looked like a family (except the father). I started to feel it then, and I really don't know why. People fucking kill. Rwanda, Sudan, it doesn't matter, people fucking kill. Stamping on the cat, that was mercy. We'd seen death so many times. Mostly, dead people look peaceful. It's the way the muscle tone goes and there comes this point where they are just 'things'. But today I felt different.

Twenty-one miles. Yep, it's definitely them. The way they run is distinctive.

This was when we found the dairy. Fucking incongruous or what? Right in the middle of it all, deep up the arse of Africa, a fucking dairy. They made fucking ice cream! The Chocolate Kingfisher Company. Here's this place, a big white building, and all along the top there are these cartoon black faces, kids enjoying ice cream, then the name 'The Chocolate Kingfisher Company' and a hand-painted Kingfisher about six feet high.

Twenty-three miles. There they are clear as day, limping along,

Sergeant Robin Fucking Hood and fucking Corporal Fucking Little John. Fair dues, the bastards have done well, considering, but then it's hot and you try running in a fucking dress or a fucking habit for twenty-six miles.

Inside the factory were these big stainless steel vats. We guessed they were for ice cream. The owner was probably in England, long-gone, but we found the foreman behind one of them, dead. This was when Robin Hood (Jack Cunningham) gets us all together.

'How many bodies we seen?'

'The family, the car-dealer, and this bloke.'

'Exactly. That's not enough.'

What Jack was saying was, we knew that out in the villages, the people would run off into the bush, and we always knew roughly how many would catch it. Mothers with too many little kids, old men, that sort of thing. But here was a small town and we'd only found nine bodies. It didn't make sense. Jack didn't like it much. Summat felt really bad.

Twenty-four miles. We are a hundred yards back and could pick off Robin Hood and Little John if we wanted to, but it's a lot more fun to track them down, save our energy.

They were out the back of the factory, between it and the dairy that must have supplied the milk. There was a big area that would have been for the lorries before the civil war.

Twenty-five miles. There are people walking, but not the Sarge and Corporal John Little. There they are, the fucking Flowerpot Men. Zebedee One and Zebedee Two, more like. Good foot, stump, good foot, stump.

51

The Blue Apples, they'd herded the whole fucking town together out the back of the factory and then sent them across that open ground. No problem except the area was laced with anti-personnel mines, those tiny little fuckers designed not to kill, just to blow a foot off and tie down the enemy with too many wounded. We were a couple of days late.

We come up behind Jack and John, and start taking the piss. 'Hop along now, you two. Hop it,' that sort of bollocks. They both ignore us, don't even turn round. They just make sure we see their raised fingers. Good foot, stump, good foot, stump, swish-swish-fucking-swish and bounce-bounce-bounce.

There were people alive in the middle of all that. The fucking animals knew they'd all have leg injuries, abdominal stuff. The best thing to do in that sort of killing field is walk on your hands so when you get unlucky and there's that little phutt, it blows your head off and you hear nothing. They knew we were coming. They knew we couldn't just walk away. Either we walked away, pretended we never found this, we shot the few still living, or someone had to go in and haul these poor fuckers out.

They've got people who volunteer to clear these evil fucking mines. There's a charity, that's who we run for. That day, Colin wanted to go in, grab the ones we could see waving, two kids, a woman with a dead baby in her arms. The Sarge said no. Colin said he wanted to. Fuck it, he said, we can't just leave.

'How wide are your stripes?' Jack Cunningham said and when Colin said something like, 'Fuck your stripes, we gorra do something,' Jack told Colin he'd shoot him in the back if he so much as took a step.

I won't forget Jack's face, the way he told me to get my fucking brother the fuck out of there. 'Do it fucking now, Jonesey,' he said, and I knew he wasn't going to listen to any arguments.

We were back with the others when we heard the shots. There were five, then a gap, then another one, and then a minute later, another.
It's that last one that fucks me every time I remember.

And now the four of us are side by side, half a mile of this miserable fucking marathon to go. Jack's suffering more than usual; his stump is playing up, John's OK but having one arm makes him run awkwardly and he gets blisters the size of eggs. Me, I got all my bits. I'm the lucky one, but twenty-six miles wearing tits, it takes a lot out of you. Colin lost a hand in Eritreia, then another one in Rwanda, but he says it's handy, he's balanced out and it doesn't fuck up his running. Time to blow these two sorry fuckers away.

So me and Colin kick on and catch and pass Jack and John. And there's the twenty-six mile marker just up ahead. Ha, old fuckers, good for fuck all. We are just grinning, coming towards the finish, congratulating ourselves, when Little Fucking John and Robin Fucking Hood come by us. Good foot, stump, good foot, stump.

I don't fucking believe it. Robbed.

'The point two!' Colin shouts. 'Never forget the fucking point two.'

OBELISK

THE FIRST TIME HE had seen her, she was the writer—he didn't know this—of a story he'd already chosen as winner in a competition. He was aware of her, but not seeing her—was her hair pulled back? Was there grey in it? Did she wear light-framed spectacles? He wasn't seeing her because one of the students in the class was a nightmare, a conference classic, a bitter wannabe who couldn't write, would never write—you need a soul to write—but could talk forever about conspiracies and rip-offs, and all those editors—no doubt including himself—who couldn't understand.

He began by trying to be nice, but this monster was eating class time. He moved to sarcasm—wasted, completely wasted. Eventually he had to call foul and suggest a meeting at another time; the class needed to get in some work.

Later, coffee, biscuits, the winner—her pseudonym was Obelisk—he leaned in close, not for intimacy but for group-sustaining politeness (but she just had to say this), and he, not for intimacy either, but the feeling was intimate, dropped an ear closer.

'You were,' she said. Her voice was sweet, almost English, almost something else, 'Incredibly kind to the old bat.'

He tried to be casual, but somehow this confidence was like a warm hand on his neck. He answered honestly.

'I didn't feel kind. I'll bet she writes cat stories.'

Obelisk laughed, 'She does, she does!'

He made small talk over coffee. Someone had cried off sick, was stuck in France, and he had a second short story competition to judge—only an old debt to repay made him torture himself like this, still in recovery from the other competition, more shorts, more so-fucking-what stories, fifteen funerals, thirteen triangles, this year's crop of child abuse, a spray of angels —one was an alien, and a dozen twist-endings so gross (the wheelchair, the narrator a cat; It was me! I killed her, I killed her!), the rest an exercise in filling paper.

He looked up once at her, she saw into him. He said: 'Why do people waste so much fucking time?'

She could have answered straight away but paused, her eyes fixed as if she were making deep decisions. Then, he guessed this later, she went for the easy answer, left as a question.

'Because the pottery class was full?'

At that moment he took his first look, not quite groaning, at the manuscript which would win the second competition, right now hating what some people thought was 'the short story'.

On Friday night, in that brief time, neither light nor dark, when everything is suspended in grey haze, two young women sit on the subway with their backs to the window. They have just had their nails done. Their hands are carefully laid along their thighs and they keep glancing down at them.

With them is a young man with a boy's tender beard. His smile is soft, his eyes red-rimmed. His gaze wavers, but somehow he manages to keep his eyes on one of the girls who tosses her hair and smiles.

Cups clinked, someone moved, and a part of him recognised it was time to go back into class. He stopped himself. To the woman who had whispered to him, Obelisk, he said: 'Write three openings, no more than a hundred words each. Tell the others, would you?'

'*Any* openings?'

'No,' he said, trying not to look down. 'The cues are *Pink*, *Friday*, and *Darkness*. I'd like you to create three totally different moods, different voices.'

'How long will you be?'

'Oh, no time at all,' he said, 'Just get started and I'll be there.'

'*Pink*, *Friday*, and *Darkness*. You sure?'

'Pink, Friday, and Darkness'll do,' he said.

They rose, shuffled away. The bitter one coughed but he managed to ignore her. The room thinned and he read again. *She is telling him about a friend who cut her hair this short—*

He is in the workshop within fifteen minutes. The 'Nails' story is very short and he reads it only twice to know it's in the prizes. When he enters, the bitter one puts up her hand and he grunts.

'Do you really want three openings?' she asks, and with a surge of gut-deep relief he says, that in her case—if she thinks it's more useful—she can just concentrate on one. When he glances up at Obelisk she is smiling but working, writing in what he now imagines will be a long, lazy, sensuous hand. For the sheer hell of it he shouts, 'We all done *Pink*?'

The workshop doesn't go that well, but it goes. Some of the group—they are all women and he doesn't like the dynamic— are serious, some want to write for women's magazines, one is a novelist but couldn't get in that class, one liked his books and wanted to sit in.

He reads some of his own work, stops and asks what this did, why that word, and one woman listening to one of his hits, 'The Keys', begins to cry at the back, trying not to make a noise. He tells the class this is what they should be aiming for. He wishes his aim was that good more often, but he's dancing now and only one in the class sees through him. Once he called himself a frightened rabbit masquerading as a baboon. Obelisk can see that, but if he had to guess he'd say she wasn't interested in baboons and would say the only good rabbit came in a pie.

He feels flip-flop, carrying the class, all bar one, utterly trans-parent to the one. The feeling both shakes and thrills him and he recognises the trap he has fallen into throughout his pathetic life where he cannot distinguish between the thing of minds, the thrill of pheromones. He knows he confuses intellect and heart, always has. Proximity and intensity for him begets attach-ment, infatuation, when what he has is a deep need to be intense. Love gives him intensity, but it is taking a while to learn that intensity does not mean love.

It's the afternoon of the first workshop, when he tells the group he has judged two competitions, the results are posted. Did they enter stories, did they want to tell him their pseudo-nyms? He isn't surprised when the woman with the grey hair tied back turns out to be Obelisk, not surprised she's a double-winner, even if he would not have said the two stories came from one writer. He can't tell her she has won, but he offers two titles as questions.

Yes, they are hers.

'Good work,' he says.

She nods and for the rest of the day their exchanges are charged. But he's older, wiser, fractionally more in control than once upon a time. His confusions are just as potent, but now he stands aside, recognising them as confusions, and mostly tran-sient. When later they drink wine, when there's a reading, all intensity, then a late heavy room, a guitar, the soft smell of spliff, women displayed on kitchen surfaces, knees up to their chins, nodding sagely, night slipping over their shoulders like a wrap, the windows mirrors, his aches—he chooses sleep and leaves for his bed, alone.

Maybe a year later he writes a story, 'Henry James Munro falls down a well':

Her name was Louise Joan Peters, a librarian, quite tall, he remembered, but somehow small, and, he thought, yes, fragile, with her quiet, gentle, whispered librarian's voice. She was forty-three (Henry was forty-seven). He had looked into her soft eyes one dusty-libraried five o'clock and said (meaning history, of course), 'May I order the 'Wistfully of Wallpaper'?'

And something happened to Henry Munro's solitary, celibate life at that moment. He developed a beautiful lisp and a desire to write poetry. He also found that the colours he began to choose, always pastel, of course, always subtle, now took on the colour of his librarian's eyes.

This amuses him. He isn't sure what it means, but didn't he teach the Dorothea Brande method—*access to the unconscious is writing* — *find out why, and when you know why, you know what, the writing will be you.*

But why he should imagine his double-winner, his whisperer (she'd gone on to better things while he trod water) like this, after so much time, he didn't know. Confusing intensities, he guessed didn't have to have a time limit.

Louise, Louise: it was strange how now, looking again, from here, from here where he could see so clearly what he had failed to quite feel then, had failed to follow through, how obvious everything now was. Henry had died believing he had never known love. But perhaps he had, once.

The way her hair was pulled back, tied into a long slack pony tail of dark blonde — once she had bent to pick up a fallen note and he had seen a silver hair clasp with romping puppies on it — and the way her smile came in two steps, a quick half-smile and then, a fuller, tooth-filled one of confession, offered vulnerability; but it was the eyes that had held him, though only now did he actually know this, how the aquamarine, the turquoise, the blue-green-to-grey, the soft, faint blurs of those windows to her aching, half-empty heart had shone, not gold, but opal, muted diamonds, her.

Oh, he thought, Louise, Louise, Louise, and he remembered how, on that last Friday — remembered — how it had ended when it had yet to begin, how Miss L. J. Peters had slipped away before he knew he needed her.

But what fascinates him when he reads his story — it won a small prize, saw daylight in a small press — what surprises him is how *chaste* the memory has become. He knows his confusions don't only mix intensities, he knows of his mistakes, back when he still buzzed madly, how he grabbed infatuations and went too far, driven by his own passion, his single-mindedness.

The difference, he decides, is simply that he is older, and when he looks at his story (which he thinks deserves a bigger audience), and he reads a little more, his chaste love mutates into sacrifice:

Now he sees a librarian's eyes, turquoise, and in them the soft-sea sweetness of hope, sees her funny two-stage smile, and he thinks about when he met her, how briefly he had felt softer, and the world not quite so brutal.

Still asleep, Frank rolls over, his thick fingers reaching for his wife. In the dark, Louise dreams too. She senses a man called Henry James Munro,

59

*and as rough hands, faintly less harsh, move on her, she imagines a soft-
ness, a little delicacy, and though, as she floats nearer to consciousness she
knows her faint pleasure is only a dream, she determines to try one last
time, to try and make things gentler.*

And his sense is almost righteousness, a satisfaction.

He is fifty-seven, but he is older. He lives now in a small Berk-
shire town through which a river, a canal, flows. He has a small
place on the edge of a forest bought with royalties from his one
big hit.

When the telephone rings and he answers, it is a woman, an
accent. She says her name is Jenny West. 'Do I—?' he asks,
croaking like an old man.

'Obelisk,' she says. She'll be passing through. Coffee?

Obelisk, he thinks, 'Painted Nails' and, and—there was a
story, a boy, his crippled sister, a fire. Oh yes.

'I judged a story.'

'Yes. I haven't long. I'm on my way to London, but if you have
time?'

He suggests a pleasant small café. They could meet there, but
it's a nice day, they could walk along the canal, it's very pretty.
He also says she should take him as she finds him. One eccen-
tricity he insists on is his tights, runners' clothing. He finds it
so comfortable he wears little else except when he has to at
awards dinners and so on—not that he wins things now.

They arrange to meet at high noon.

Her hair is all silver now, though she is barely fifty, her face a
little harder, but of course she is Obelisk, the promising writer,
the double-winner, the—*The way her hair was pulled back, tied into
a long slack pony-tail of dark blonde*—once she had bent to pick up a

fallen note and he had seen a silver hair-clasp with romping puppies on it—and the way her smile came in two steps, a quick half-smile and then, a fuller, tooth-filled one of confession, offered vulnerability; but it was the eyes that had held him, though only now did he actually know this, how the aquamarine, the turquoise, the blue-green-to-grey, the soft, faint blurs of those windows to her aching, half-empty heart had shone, not gold but opal, muted diamonds, her.

As they walk the canal, past newly-painted barges with flower-displays, he is conscious, almost self-conscious of his dress. Perhaps he's a little old to prance about in Lycra. He still runs four miles a day, but now he is a leisure runner, no longer competitive.

Jenny talks pleasantly. She has won things, then a big prize in Canada, the collection of shorts. Yes, 'Nails' is in there and 'Jake's Barn', then the novel and her short-list for the Governor General's Prize (no, Alice Munro again).

And how is he?

He answers, as truthfully as he can. He still teaches, he says, but everything is still so-fucking-what, there is no *soul*, no heart, no sex. No one bleeds. Perhaps he's sounding bitter, but it isn't bitterness he feels, more *waste*. In the past ten years he has watched the world become yet more glib, the Booker panel filled by celebrities, new short story writers, slick girls and pretty boys. Then suddenly he remembers the bitter old witch, the wannabe conspiracy theorist. Did Jenny know the old bat had fallen down some stairs and sued the college?

'You were so kind to her,' Jenny says. 'I thought you were a saint.'

He stops as she walks ahead. 'Oh, God no,' he says.

SPECTACLES, TESTICLES, WALLET & WATCH

LATE FEBRUARY, 1991. FRIDAY

FRIDAY AFTERNOON, VERY COLD, and Tom Smith, sales manager, leaves his London offices for home. Tom has left a little early. Once a week he allows himself the chance to beat the crush of commuters travelling from Waterloo to the South Coast. He knows that the 15:30 train to Weymouth will be at worst three-quarters full, and that the one after that won't have an empty seat. Tom hates to board anything later. He knows that any train after 15:45 will be little better than a cattle truck.

As Tom walks across Waterloo Bridge he rehearses a new joke, one he heard today at lunch. The wind off the Thames is vicious, but Tom's eyes shine and he walks on. December was his first million-pound month and tomorrow his sales force are coming to a party to celebrate. That's why Tom wants to remember the joke. He chants the punchline almost like a mantra. Tom is 33.

While Tom Smith mutters and smiles despite the wind, in Amman, Jordan, Mohammed El-Hassi Siddiqi, 34, a physician, from Basra, Iraq, is just boarding a Jordanian 747 bound for London Heathrow Airport. El-Hassi is wrapped against the early evening chill and shivers, but it is not because of the cold. El-Hassi is scared of flying. As the jumbo begins to roll, he prays.

Tom and El-Hassi are carrying briefcases and they both carry paperback books to read on their journey. When El-Hassi was studying in England he became a fan of the thriller writer Dick Francis. He has *Reflex* to read on the flight, and is pleased, knowing he should finish it before the plane lands in London.

Tom Smith used to read every new Dick Francis, but now thinks life's too short. He is carrying *Winning by Intimidation* and a collection of poetry from soldiers of the Great War.

Tom and El-Hassi travel west. They do not know each other, nor will they ever see or touch each other, but they are destined to meet the following Monday in dark, unusual and desperate circumstances. On the jumbo jet, El-Hassi drinks orange juice and reads his novel. On the express to Southampton, Tom first tries to read the business book, snaps it shut, then tries the poetry. But he can't concentrate or get in the right mood. He drinks a second Bells & American to take the edge off the nagging ache in his gut.

SATURDAY, EVENING

'Spectacles, testicles, wallet and watch!' Tom crosses himself as he cracks the joke, forehead, abdomen, shoulder, shoulder. The party is going very well, all his reps are well-oiled and most of them are laughing. The wives are in the kitchen sorting out the crispy stuff. Someone shouts, waving a glass.

'Christ, Tom, You're a bloody heathen, you know that?'

'Oh, that reminds me,' Tom says. He's had a few too. 'Did you hear the one about the bishop and the salesman playing golf?'

Tom's wife Susan comes in, leading a procession of women

and plates of food. The men are laughing, but Susan is not amused. 'You promised, Tom.'

Tom looks forlorn. 'OK. OK!' he says. 'Who fancies some karaoke?'

A thin woman with dark eyes and black hair looks for her husband's face. The husband, Mike, Tom's top salesman, sees her and he shakes his head briefly. Susan sees this. She puts down her plates and smiles. 'Don't worry, Siobhan. Tom will be good now I'm here.' Siobhan doesn't speak, but relaxes very slightly.

Someone turns up the karaoke machine and starts singing 'You're The One That I Want'. Tom grins and crunches into a piece of celery.

Later, Tom and one of the guys are drunk and they try to render their version of 'New York! New York!', kicking their legs high, but rapidly losing touch with the words. At some point they fall together and demolish a glass coffee table. They think it's hilarious, but neither of the wives laughs.

Later still, Tom: 'So, the salesman misses another putt, and of course he says, 'Fuck it! I missed!' again, and the bishop looks up to the heavens and this time the sky does open up, just like he had warned it would, and a mighty hand appears and a finger points, and a huge bolt of lightning flashes to the earth, and, and . . . kills the bishop!'

He pauses, swigs half a glass of wine, 'And a great voice booms out . . .'

From the men there is a shouted chorus of 'Fuck it, I missed!'

Susan is unhappy. She has seen Siobhan's dark face. It is not the time to remind Tom of his resolution. Instead she complains, 'Tom, that is so old.'

'I know,' Tom says. 'Lapsed Catholic and a failed comedian.'

'Yes,' Susan says sharply. She is picking up some dirty plates.

64

'Anyway, you shouldn't, especially not with Mike and Siobhan here.'

Tom seems surprised. 'Mikey's OK.'

'They are both church-goers, Tom. It wouldn't hurt for you to try.'

Tom stops. He thinks; then he speaks slowly. 'You're right, love. I'll try to remember.' He nods to Siobhan, then nods to Mike. Then as if it had never happened, he turns to the party. 'Hey, who wants some crisps?'

Later still, Tom has forgotten, and after some shop talk with a manager down from Leeds, he acts out the one about Jesus Christ nailed to the cross, showing off his miraculous powers, first pulling away one hand, then the other, then toppling forward, still nailed by the feet. Mike and Siobhan are putting their coats on as he tells the joke. Siobhan is flushed with anger and hurt, Mike is sad and embarrassed. Tom doesn't see. As they are leaving, he slaps Mike's back and congratulates him again for being his top salesman.

Mike sighs, then leans towards his boss, friend, and whispers. 'Tom you're a good mate and a good bloke. You don't have to be a idiot, you know.'

Tom shrugs, 'Someone's gotta do it, Mikey. I ain't no saint.'

Tom shakes Mike's hand which is strong and firm. Siobhan, he kisses lightly on a cool cheek, and then they are gone. He goes back to the party.

The night winds down. A few people smoke. They drink coffee, talk about the war just won in the Gulf. Tom had found it harrowing. He cares about the deaths, the clinical accuracy of smart bombs, the fate of the Kurds; he was disgusted by the film of the carnage on the road to Basra. Someone agrees and likens it to Hiroshima, mass-killing as a political statement. For some

65

reason all this talk makes Tom think of his writing, the poetry in his desk, the snippet in his briefcase, the two half-finished novels stored away somewhere.

Suddenly Tom feels the minor cut on his hand from the accident earlier and now things are winding down he sees and hears the brash crowd he has surrounded himself with, the crowd he created, that he plays at being part of. His stomach lurches and he has to shake his head. Then he makes a dash for the safer ground of flippancy, cracking some silly remark.

'Hey, we won, didn't we?' someone says. 'You're not saying we shouldn't have gone in are you? I mean the guy was another Hitler, wasn't he?'

'There are ways,' Susan says softly, 'and there are limits.' Then the guy from Leeds says they are only talking about a bunch of Arabs.

'Oh, God!' Susan says. 'I think it's time I went to bed!'

Tom is lying there now, his small bedside lamp light-blue beside him, the book of war poetry in his hand. Susan's back is hunched and cold. She is facing away from him and her light is out. He feels wretched.

'Susan?' he says, staring at the ceiling. There is no answer. 'Susan,' he says, 'd'you think I'm an idiot?'

'Go to sleep.'

'Look,' he says, 'just answer me, OK? Am I? Am I an idiot?'

Susan still faces away. 'Well, you're not a racist like that Jack Harvey.'

'No,' Tom says. 'But Mike said something when he was leaving.'

'Will you go to sleep!'

Tom feels like crying. 'Just tell me, Suze . . .'

66

Susan rolls over. She comes up on one elbow. She breathes once, deep.

'Tom, I married you because I loved you, and God knows I still love you. You're funny and you're not selfish—the reps don't know what you do for them, or what you've given up, but I do. And I love your writing, Tom. Scrub that—when you wrote, I loved your writing. We're rich, and we call this happy. But ages ago I told you, I told you I'd rather you were writing and us poor. You didn't believe me. So, yes, you're an idiot.'

'Oh,' Tom says. He thinks he's about to say something profound, maybe even mention his new poem. Instead he says, 'I suppose this means a fuck is out of the question?'

'Yes,' Susan says. She rolls away, but then Tom kisses her shoulder, not sexually but to say thank you. He puts down his book and looks up at the ceiling again. Susan keeps her eyes closed and her back turned, but she reaches behind her until she can touch him. Eventually Tom sleeps.

SUNDAY

In the morning, hungover, Tom gets up, dresses, goes out and drives to the forest. He is a long-distance runner and he is meeting his friends for their two-hour Sunday run. They set off and he drops in alongside a gentle giant called Peter, a rock, a family man and a good Catholic.

'You're a left footer, aren't you, Pete, a Roman Candle?'

Peter grunts, the pace is hard on him.

'So am I,' Tom says, almost apologising. 'Once upon a time, the whole shebang, The Nine Fridays, Ash Wednesday, Palm

67

Sunday, Corpus Christi, everything. I was even an altar boy for a while.'

Peter grunts again.

'I knew my Catechism off by heart, too! Who made you? God made me! Why did God make you? God made me to know him, love him and serve him, in this world and the next.'

Another grunt.

'I knew it all, mate. I was a devout little bugger. Then one day it stopped. I don't know why. Suddenly it seemed like so much bullshit, stuff to keep the masses in line.'

Peter finally speaks. The words are gasped. 'You gotta have something.'

'Probably,' Tom says.

'Y'need a reason. Otherwise, what do we bother for?'

'Don't see it.'

'Sense've purpose, then.'

'What's wrong with just living?' Tom says.

'You tell me,' Peter says. 'You asked the questions.'

Tom goes quiet. He runs easily, thinking without words. He can sense and smell the peculiar moment before the words of a poem begin to appear. Peter's breath is laboured and Tom knows he is staying with the pace out of politeness. To let him off the hook he says something sarcastic then kicks hard to catch the front runners. Running this fast he feels exalted. He glories in the sense of his own body, the power, the air in his face, the frozen earth under his feet, the stark trees, distant horses grazing. His problems float away. Vaguely he thinks of a meeting in London tomorrow, talk of a partnership, a meeting in a hotel on Piccadilly. When he catches the guys at the front he tells them a joke and drops into step.

MONDAY

Somewhere between Saturday evening and the early hours of Monday, Susan has seized her chance, and when Tom comes downstairs on Monday morning there is a small folder next to his briefcase. Tom recognises it straight away and with a tiny shiver, sees his own handwriting, 'This Time!' across it in a thick bold red pen. He knows precisely what is in the light-green envelope. 'Evidence I have Travelled'?

Susan nods.

'Why now?' Tom says.

'Because you're ready,' Susan says.

Tom has come down to breakfast psyched-up, ready for one more week as a sales manager. He is glass and steel; he is cold and hard. He is not a poet or a writer of prose this morning. He is neither warmth nor wood, nor grass, nor water and he is not heart, and not soul. Instead he is what he thinks he must be: hard-headed, get-ahead, efficient. Susan should have tried this move after Tom's Sunday run when she knows he is always mellow and at his most receptive, not now. Tom knows his next move is to be angry, so he picks up the stuff and manages not to say anything else.

Susan pours a little coffee for Tom, then listens to Today on Radio 4. When Tom is about to leave to catch the 7:08 to London, they properly kiss. Apart from this thing with the writing, they both know everything is all right. Tom is aroused by the warmth of Susan's kiss and he realises it's been ten days. He thinks, when they met, when they met . . . and then, ah, what the hell. He kisses her again and leaves for work. Susan watches his back, watches him climb into his sports car and drive away. She waits until she can no longer hear the engine. It's very cold, frost and ice on the road. When she is certain she can no longer hear her husband, she goes inside their house, switches off the radio and sits down with a mug of coffee and his poems. She thinks they need a holiday, a few days somewhere warm and quiet.

Eleven minutes later, at two minutes past seven, Tom is parking his car at Southampton Parkway railway station. As Susan drinks her third coffee and reads another poem, Tom steps on to the platform. It's busy of course, and everyone is wrapped up against the cold. Susan pops two rounds of bread into the toaster as the London train pulls into the station. She no longer thinks of the mechanics of her husband's journey, just the train times.

07:08

Tom travels in the buffet car. He sips a coffee. The usual crowd is on the train—commuters, creatures of habit—a bridge game in one corner, the rest reading. Tom could read anything, but he doesn't read his manuscript. When it nags at him he tucks it away in the lid of his briefcase. He thinks, maybe on the way back down, if he can get a seat. The train rocks, clatters, racing to London, fields and fences whipping past the windows.

08:12

There is no screech of brakes, no squeal of wheels, no cries of despair. There is just the bang.

The noise has barely registered; Tom's first sensation is of being on a ship at sea. His table moves and he is earthless and choking, falling backwards, while the table, other things, he

70

thinks, fly softly in the opposite direction. He has a moment where he wonders if perhaps these seconds are special and he thinks of the six o'clock news and there is red and he sleeps.

He regains consciousness in a dark, dark jungle with branches all around him. He can hear snakes, zithering, hissering, slithering along a wishy, silly floor. He thinks of water. Somewhere he hears something which he thinks of as crackling, then he becomes quiet again.

He wakes the second time and feels Susan lying heavily across his thighs, fast asleep. When he goes to move her she is hard and flat and wide and he feels fear. Susan? He is somewhere dark and he hurts. His eyes are sore and he thinks he can hear or smell water. He tries to sit up and feels terrific pain. He lets out a groan and then someone says, faintly, 'Hello?'

Tom is cold, numb, so terribly frightened that he does not answer. Then the voice whispers again, 'Hello?'

It is a tiny, fragile voice, and foreign. Tom cannot feel or sense where it is. He thinks of up and down and left and right, but in the darkness, in this thing, this crush that holds him, he isn't even sure where up is. He decides to speak. When he does, his dry mouth has difficulty forming a word. Eventually he croaks to the darkness and it replies, 'Hello?'

He hears the fragile voice, he thinks below him, but in the black the words float and he isn't sure. He is hesitant. He still does not understand what has happened. For some reason he thinks he's in hospital, dreaming under an anaesthetic. But gradually an older part of Tom remembers. 'My name is Tom,' he says. 'You?'

'My name is El-Hassi.'

'I can't quite hear you,' he says, 'or where you are. What was your name again?'

From a different place, like something scurrying he hears the name again and he asks again, 'Did you say El-Hassi?'

'Yes. I am Arab.'

'Arab?'

'I am from Iraq.'

Now Tom remembers—he was travelling, the hotel, the bang, the sudden puff, things changing shape, the falling, the dark.

'Listen,' Tom says. 'This might sound silly, but could you keep talking? I can't work out where you are. If you keep talking, I can zero in on you.'

Suddenly he thinks of a smart bomb striking a bunker.

'I am here,' says the quiet voice. 'What would you like me to say?'

'I don't know, mate, anything. Sing a song for all I care.'

'Be calm,' says the quiet, foreign voice. Then El-Hassi begins to chant, reminding Tom of the monotony of the rosary, but sounding more real.

'*La ilaha ilal Lah. La ilaha ilal Lah. La ilaha ilal Lah.*'

It is to Tom's right, close, quite close, below him or above him.

'*La ilaha ilal Lah. La ilaha ilal Lah. La ilaha ilal Lah.*'

To his right. Quite close. Maybe slightly above him.

'I've got you, mate! You can stop now.'

But the man continues, merely quieter, '*La ilaha ilal Lah.*' And the sound soothes Tom and then his focus improves, he hears noises, water, and begins to think the blackness has variations. Tom likes the chant.

'Are you hurt, mate? Are you OK?'

'I think I am hurt, but it does not matter. I am all right, I think.'

72

'Are you trapped? I'm stuck under something, a girder I think. I can't move anything.'

'I am also under things, friend. I cannot feel my legs now and I think one of my arms is broken.'

Tom tries to move, but it is impossible. The discomfort makes him groan. 'Shit, mate, you seem pretty cool, you must be in pain.'

'A little.'

'Aren't you frightened?'

The voice is soft. 'Frightened? No. What is writ is writ. I am at peace.'

'Is that your chant thing? What is it, Buddhist?'

'*La ilaha ilal Lah.* There is no God but Allah.'

'Well, I don't know about that, mate, but it's got a lovely sound to it.'

There were different shades of blackness around them now. Up, at least what Tom thought was up, was slightly lighter, approaching a dark grey, and over to his far left, was a medium-dark grey, cast with what he thought was a reflected lighter grey like a low-powered moon on a miserable night.

'Do you know what happened, mate?'

'No. I was travelling to London. I am a little confused.'

Tom thinks, Jesus, the train . . .

'Can you see anything?'

'Just a little, friend, but I think things are clearer.'

'I think I'm still in my chair,' Tom says. 'We must have hit something. I was in the buffet when it happened.'

'I was in the buffet, also. Allah was with us, do you think? We are perhaps underneath some of the buffet. I cannot see or move to see, but I think so.'

Something in the voice.

73

'Are you all right?'

'Oh, I am sorry, my friend. No, I do not think I am all right. I feel wet and I am getting weaker, I think. I will be late for an appointment.'

Tom is feeling closed in, frightened, but suddenly this seems too funny. 'You're joking, right?'

'Yes, my friend.'

Tom speaks to the darkness. 'What was your name again? El-hassi wasn't it? How many people—what do you think—I mean . . .'

'I do not know, friend, and I am sad, but this must have been what Allah wished. Our lives are God's.'

Tom tries to move and again the pain stops him.

'Give me a minute,' he says.

He had been in the buffet. He was thinking about his writing.

'El-hassi,' he asks thoughtfully, 'When did you realise?'

'I did not. I was first aware when I awoke.'

'But it's a train wreck, right? Why is it so dark?'

'I think we are beneath some wood, perhaps the buffet bar. It is this which has spared us so far.'

'So far?'

'Oh, yes. If you listen, you can hear the emergency services. But they are quite a way above us. I think perhaps we may have to wait a while.'

'They'll think we're dead . . .'

'They will be thorough.'

'We could shout. Bang on a girder or something.'

'Yes, we could my friend, but I would rather not.'

'Jesus Christ, why not?'

'You blaspheme. But I understand, you are worried. You must

74

make your own choices. I already have made mine. I do not wish to divert the rescue services to help me. They will come to us when they are ready. I do not think Allah wishes me to think selfishly. If this is an end it is fitting.'

'Jesus!'

'Was an important prophet, a messiah, but not the son of God.'

'Jesus!'

'There is only one God and his prophet is Mohammed.'

'Jesus!'

'La ilaha ilal Lah.' Quieter.

'El-Hassi, you married, any kids?'

'Yes, I have a son, seven.'

'Susan can't have any. We lost one, it would've been a boy. He would be about seven now.'

El-Hassi doesn't answer. His voice has been getting weaker.

Tom closes his eyes. He thinks of his time as an altar boy, how everything then was rote, ritual, how the Latin responses to the priest were just sounds, melodies like El-Hassi's. And he thinks of the smell of incense, then smells the forest pine of his runs, and he senses the deep warmth of Susan. Suddenly he wishes that they had made love on Saturday night. He feels like crying, not for himself, but at the thought of Susan, a policeman approaching her door.

And Tom realises there's a danger he might think seriously about life and maybe an approaching death or two and he remembers his refuge in idiocy. He calls out to El-Hassi who says, 'Yes?' but faintly. Tom suddenly thinks it's his duty to divert his fellow victim from sleep. He thinks it will be more than sleep. 'So El-Hassi,' he says, 'what does your name mean?'

'What?'

'What does your name mean? Me, I'm Doubting Thomas.'

'I do not know, my friend but *hass* is to feel or touch, to sense.'

Touch? Seems about right. Right now, Tom wouldn't mind reaching out and touching this bloke's hand, but he can't. He thinks about telling the spectacles, testicles joke, but it's too dark and would be wasted on the Iraqi, and anyway, Tom can't move his arms. Tom feels frustrated.

'This God of yours, El, what's the score? I mean, what's so wrong with God the Father, God the Son, and God the Holy Ghost?'

'There is only one God, my friend.'

'Yeah, and he wears a gold crown and his son has a big red heart sticking out of his chest; oh, and sometime he's a bird, but I never really got that bit.'

El-Hassi barely grunts but Tom thinks it might have been a laugh.

'So, if we had to bet right now, what d'you reckon, El, your God or mine?'

'Allah knows me, friend. If you like, we can use yours.'

'I'm trying to be funny, El.'

'I know, my friend.'

Tom feels an odd peace and he decides what will be will be. He still has the urge, though, to reach out to touch this Arab, and he would like to cross himself once, just in case, spectacles, testicles, wallet and watch. But he can't move. He laughs. 'Hey, El, I sure wish I could move these fucking arms. I know a few jokes, but they need actions, you know?'

There is no answer, but Tom keeps talking. He tells El-Hassi how awful he thought the killings were on the road to Basra. He talks about running, he describes every man in the running club, his best race, the day he broke the club record for a half-marathon. But the answers stop coming and he hears the sounds of people above him, the crackle of acetylene torches, controlled shouting. He decides to tell his friend about his writing, his dreams. He knows now that he should survive this. He has things to do. He thinks he needs a holiday with Susan, a few days somewhere warm and quiet.

He wants to write.

THE LAST LOVE LETTER OF BERWYN PHILIP PRICE

Price, Berwyn Philip. b: 11.2.1921, d: 12.2.1997.
Wing and full-back, (occasionally scrum-half). Played, Aberavon (267), Barbarians (3), Wales (42). 'B.P.', Known for his blistering pace, scored 27 tries for Wales, most notably the two tries in injury time in 'B.P.'s Triumph' the 1947 21-20 win over England at Twickenham. Also representative honours, Wales 100/220 yards. Empire Games Gold Medal, 1948 (100yds) Son of Philip Price, Swansea & Aberavon, one Welsh cap.

MRS BETHAN PRICE, IF you're reading this, then it looks like I must have managed it, after all. I went and over-did it and popped my clogs, just like you and Doctor Llewellyn said I would. Bugger me, I'm dead, well what do you know? I'm sorry love, but if that's what happened, then it happened. I'll bet I died happy, though. Was it at the Arms Park? I bet all I could see when the moment finally came was red and white and green. I bet I could smell the lads and the mud, see the flags and hear, 'Bread of Heaven'!

I bloody well hope it was like that. I hope I didn't keel over on the way to the stadium. You and the girls, Pimple Thomas, Ivor, Bernard, all the lads, you might've missed the game, I couldn't have had that. That's why I had the little note behind my leek and pinned to my collar. I left this letter here for you, but the note was something else. That was why I made you promise.

Oh, my darling woman, I'm going to miss you. I think you'll

be glad of a rest though, eh? All the talk about rugby and me never letting you forget that you gave me four daughters when I wanted a few more Price boys to carry on the family name. Oh, Bethan Price, I hope you'll forgive me. I know you wanted me to be a quiet old man, but I just couldn't do it. In the end, God knows best. He knows more than doctors and nurses and reporters and people from the television. After waiting twenty-nine years, do you honestly think I could have missed the game? Do you really think I could have missed a Price boy on the wing, a Price at scrum-half, and, bugger me, a Price grandson playing for England against us? Love, I think I wanted to die at the game. I think I knew nothing would ever be better than that Saturday.

But I am sorry, love, I know it was a little selfish. But I think, all in all, it was better like that, better than to fade away slowly. Dylan Thomas got close to what I mean. I couldn't go gentle, mun, not me, not B.P. Price.

> Old age should burn and rave at close of day;
> Rage, rage against the dying of the light.

Oh, Beth, my lover, try to laugh. Do you remember how hard we had to fight to get tickets? We had our debentures, but we had to get tickets for all the old boys, for Gwyneth's family, the Evanses, Tommy Thomas, Pimple and Argus and a pair for Jones-Eighteen-months! All that bloody wheeling and dealing! I should have been done in well before the game, but that would've been a bit cruel and I didn't think your God in Heaven was like that. I think, deep inside, I knew I'd make it to kick-off, just as I was pretty sure I wouldn't be watching any more games, at least not from our seats in the stand.

79

It's funny, but I was never really scared of dying. I never thought of it, hardly, but the first time I did was when I won my Empire Games medal.

Four years I'd worked for that. Ivor Coach Jenkins from Cardiff A.C. had trained me and I worked, oh, Beth, how I worked for that extra half second, then that extra tenth of a second, and then the dip that got me home from that good black chappie, Tomkins. Under ten seconds for the hundred yards, Beth! That's not bad now, but then it was a bloody miracle! We were on cinders and wearing what we called lightweight spikes. Compared to nowadays we were running in hob-nailed boots. And I ran nine-nine, Beth, nine-point-nine, and they put a ribbon round my neck and a big gold medal.

But there was a moment then, when I thought about dying. There's a point in a race when you're flying, when you're an angel, just before it really hurts — you're on another level and all the rules are different and you are so special, so damn-well Godly, and you just know something is out there.

Being so alive like that, well, it makes you wonder about things, about dying too. But it's a nice feeling, Beth, not a bad one.

I remember when you gave birth to Gwyneth. I admit I was disappointed. I admit it, I wanted a boy, but you, all the pain you'd just had, love, and you looked into my eyes and you smiled. you'd done your nine-nine for the hundred too, you'd been there, and it was in your face. I think I was playing for Aberavon then, I scored a few tries, and the next season I got my first cap for Wales.

Oh, Beth, do you remember? We had those four tickets for Murrayfield and a hotel booking, and I tried to trade them with

E. Briscoe Phillips for his two England tickets. Then the cheeky bugger wanted us to throw in his coach fare to Edinburgh as well, d'you remember? And in the end we had to give E. Briscoe our Parc des Princes tickets too, but only when he let us have his three tickets for the Ireland game. Bloody bloke, everything the hard way. He must make love standing up in a hammock and take his goldfish walking.

Still, we got our tickets, didn't we? Oh, I do hope you can see the funny side. I hope you're not all tearful and saying 'If we'd not got the tickets . . .'

What was the deal for Jones-Eighteen-Months, can you remember? It was so bloody complicated! He gave us thirty-five quid up front, didn't he, and then he said he'd fit Mrs Gill Williams' kitchen. Then Mrs Gill Williams lent her one-ton van to Dai Rees, and for that Dai said we could have the two tickets if we'd let him use the caravan at Trecco Bay a couple of week-ends. Whisht, I'm thinking maybe E. Briscoe's deal wasn't that complicated after all.

Don't go thinking the tickets were a mistake, love. They weren't. Think of the view I'm getting now, and bugger their debentures!

But I will miss you, Bethan Price, and I do feel guilty for leaving you alone. Life and death is funny, you know. I want to say hurry up so we can be together again, but then if I was there for your birthday, I'd be singing, 'Many happy returns!' Daft, eh?

I'm too old to pretend I didn't want boys, but I ought to say, Beth, I really ought to say that the girls lit up my life. God, Bethan, the four of them are so beautiful, like you are, and all so fiery, and who would have thought they'd marry the family back into rugby and I'd get to see three grandsons at the

81

National Stadium before I took an early bath?

I'm not unhappy, Beth, love. Really. It's a funny sort of happy-sad that's not easy to pin down, but it's definitely not a bad feeling. I might be getting religion right on the final whistle, but I think it's just the thought of seeing John, Matt and Iestyn running out there. Oh, please, God, don't let me die before I see the boys touch the turf.

You're downstairs now, in the kitchen, making ham rolls for the game and a flask of oxtail soup. The house is so quiet, I can hear it breathing and then, faintly, if I listen hard, you humming as you prepare our half-time snap. You always said you didn't hum, but you did, Beth.

I'm hiding in the office, Beth, surrounded by all the books, scratching this to you, thinking of all the time you gave to me, how you gave me four daughters and a tribe of grand-children and every last one with either your red hair and green eyes, our love for words, or a few—not that many, but just enough— with the good Price hands and the fast Price feet, two of them, two, good enough to play for Wales, and one to play for England. That really is odd, but he's a good number eight, as good as they've had for twenty years.

And Gwyneth's little Ben the best of all, on that wing, eight years old, living, breathing for his rugby, and is he fast!

I'd write more, Bethan, but the longer I stay up here the longer I'm without you. You always said I spent too long in here, marking papers, working on other people's dreams. I'll finish and come downstairs, then. For one last time, I want to watch you in the kitchen, smell bread, ham, see you spread Branston and lick your fingers, see you fill your apron.

Oh, my darling woman, I am going to miss you.

82

Bethan Price puts down the letter. Part of her is roaring with joy, but there are tears rolling down her face. She can hear voices elsewhere and they are not unhappy; they ripple like a clear spring in the mountains. There are so many people, so many people, in the other room, in the hall, the kitchen, and in two marquees on the lawn, there are so many people all talking rugby and writing and still arguing about the winning English try last Saturday.

Bethan blows her nose and wipes her face. There is a glass case in one corner of Berwyn's office, somewhere, covered in manuscripts, a few match programmes. In it, a sorry leather-flecked ball scratched with faded names, English, Welsh, fine young hands, the old fingers now of fading lights, and not a few, like Berwyn, passed on, throwing a ball around in a better place, injury-free, playing with spirit, a little faster than they were, just a little braver.

Bethan takes out the ball. It's the size of a new born baby, and, she thinks briefly, skin, and capable of being so much, meaning so much more than what it is, should you simply measure things and pretend they are physical.

Beth has seen blood and mud, seen the scarves fly, the foam rubber leeks waved, the coaches in convoys going up the M5, along the M4, to Scotland, to Twickenham HQ. Bethan has gone to Cardiff airport to fly to Dublin and gone there with Berwyn to fly to Paris. Once they travelled to the other side of the world to watch brave Welsh boys crushed by farmers dressed in black. Bethan has seen every mad celebration, and every rain-beaten temporary depression, and she has heard every argument, every explanation and one thousand and one excuses. And she always shook her head and always said, 'Boys, it's only a game, only a game.'

She holds the ball like Berwyn might have, then crooked into her elbow like a baby, then like a wing, flying down the line, his boot studs an inch from the white lime edge of touch, his eyes gleaming, so near to being, well, Godly, at the height of living and touching the hem of death.

And she dabs her face again, takes a huge deep breath, then another, goes to the wall where Berwyn's gold medal hangs and looks in the mirror there. She takes out her compact and tidies herself up a bit, for Berwyn's sake, for the girls, the lads.

They had got home late after the game, almost eight o'clock, and Berwyn was still red-faced, bursting with the afternoon's höel and magic. He couldn't stop talking about Iestyn's try, the way John had virtually run the game for Wales from behind the scrum. Even the last-minute winner scored by Philip Price, the English number eight, couldn't dampen the light in Berwyn's eyes. In the pub he had drunk his second brandy and laughed with an English couple that the team in white couldn'ta done it without that sprinkling of Welsh blood. The best English player was a *Price*, for God's sake!

Berwyn had been quiet in the car on the way home, then in a reflective moment he had said, 'Beth, you think young Ben will pull on the red shirt?'

When they had come in, Berwyn had taken off his coat and unpinned the leek from the collar and the note had fallen out. He had picked it up and laughed. It was something about dealing with him at half-time, he'd said, or full-time, but not missing the match. *You promised*, it said on the bottom. He had sat down then, still chuckling, and Bethan had gone to make some tea. Berwyn never got to drink it.

Bethan looks in the mirror and she decides she looks OK. She picks up the rugby ball and goes out, downstairs. She can hear the video recording of the game being played again, far too loudly, and then she hears a taped roar and someone shouts, 'Yes! Yes!' and she hears 'Bread of Heaven'.

(Please note the almanac entry is fictional.)

THE BASTARD WILLIAM WILLIAMS

I AM THE BASTARD William Williams, late of The Universal Pit, Senghennydd, then Abertridwr, and latterly the cellars of The Commercial Hotel, as pot man. Now that the dust have slowed me I am easy to find. I am still lived next door to the English Congregational Church, Commercial Road, Senghennydd. I venture from my place only for the English Cong, and in summer, if I am lucky, a visit from a relation.

Until the coal dust on my chest confined me to my front room, I have been known as a hearty man. My years is matched exact to the century and for the most part it have been a good life, wholesome. I think though, with what have passed, I shall not like to be here when the clock strike two thousand.

I am fixed, I am settled; and I am Welsh! And I am proud of it, even if the English woman, Thatcher have all but killed this valley, taken away the good black-fingered work of the men; made drug addicts of our young, the men unemployed, drunkard, or gone from the valley. So easily they have forgot Rorke's Drift, forgot the five hundred and twenty men of 1901 and 1913, forgot the Great War, forgot the South Wales Borderers, never mind that they have forgot good King Henry and his Welsh boys and the hiding we did give the frogs for them at Agincourt.

We are nothing, see, statistics is it, and a long way from London.

I am not one for writing, and never was much of a one for talking either. I would not tell you of this, I would just let it go, but Lord forgive me, I am writing it down. I have a good copperplate strapped into me at town school which has never left me; I have my retirement pen, my Quink, a pad to write this and enough hot in me to bore a new pitshaft. I must record the visit of the man Allen Jones. If I am not to get this out of me, I will surely be bursted, so better or worse, it shall go down.

Allen Jones, with long red hair like a woman, a liking for his own voice and him on a fired-up mission to discover his past. A writer, he said he was, and without a by-your-leave or a telephone message did he turn up here, all mouth and trousers and flashing teeth to ask of me questions, one hundred miles an hour, and then to tell me about Senghennydd, to tell me about the boys. And I tell you, no warning, just one day, knock-knock on my door.

'Mr Williams?'

He do smile at me, condescending, like an English Member of Parliament or some social worker have come to see I am washed.

'I am William Williams, yes. The Council, is it?'

He has the smile again. His teeth do remind me of Robert Jones, the Deacon of the English Cong who married my mother. His hand is out.

'My name is Allen Jones,' says he. 'I think we are slightly related.'

'Do you now?' says I. I have not shook his hand for I feel him impolite.

'I was wondering,' he says. 'Could come in for a chat, please?'

A chat, is it? 'I am expecting a friend for tea,' says I.

'Why, even better!' says this Allen Jones. 'You see, I am

researching my family tree and I've just found out that my great-grandfather and your mother were—'

'What is it?' I have said too quickly.

'Married,' says he now, but surprised. 'After my great-grand-mother died.'

'You have done a little reading,' says I. I am turned and walking to my room and this Allen Jones, a relation is it, he have followed, but unsure of his self. I am slightly glad of this.

I have sat and Mister Allen Jones have sat and he have opened a fancy briefcase and took out a machine. I have asked Mr Jones, 'What is this for?' and he have smiled again and said to me this is a machine that it is to record all the things we say.

'What are the Commandments?' ask I. 'What is Magna Carta? What is American Declaration of Independence?'

Allen Jones begins to misunderstand me. He knows these things. Am I wanting him to say the Commandments?

'They were writ,' says I, 'without machines. Put your fangle away.'

Mr Allen looks, but I look sterner, and he puts his recorder back.

Allen Jones then have shrugged his weak shoulders and have sat forward. 'My father was Thomas Allen Jones,' he have said, 'son of Allen Thomas Jones and Caroline, the daughter of Robert Jones, and Bessie, born Milton.'

'You have the teeth of the deacon,' says myself, 'but your face is long and thin and the jaw is Bessie's. Caroline took the name Kitty. She was fair and fine, long of the face, and she sang like an angel.'

'She did?' Mr Jones is excited and he scribbles something.

'Will you like tea?' says I. I am getting up.

'Yes, yes,' Mr Jones says. He is light in the voice, sing-song like the mother of his father. He has the air of a man never married, as Oscar Wilde perhaps. I am thinking that his eyes are his finest feature, quite a blue, and his fingers are long and delicate. He lisps faintly.

'Then I will mash a pot,' says I.

He writes down 'mash'. His script is sharp and large, Catholic school italic, but fast and gestured as if his mark come out, as if he display himself as he scratches. But he is bold, I guess.

I take the caddy down and take out some Glengettie, and as the kettle come to popple, I warm the pot on the gas. I hear Allen Jones enter. He is softly spoken.

'My father did that,' says he, 'and his father.'

I am thinking maybe this is not impolite, that Allen Thomas has just little in the way of rules. The hand he writes in is him perhaps. It is an eagerness not a rudeness in him, but seen often the wrong way.

'Twice a half of two-and-a-half,' I fire quickly at him.

Allen Jones laughs. 'Two and a half!'

'Quick in school?' ask I.

'And always one eye through the window,' he says.

And Kitty too, I am thinking. She have needed room for her voice and her little poems. Tables and alphabet cluttered her. My mother was not like that.

Allen do not take sugar in his tea and only a little milk please. He have said to me he have not tasted tea like this for a long time and I have said this is just ordinary valley tea mashed proper and served in decent china. He have nodded and I see his eyes are like a butterfly around my room. He have seen the picture rail, the dado, the sepia pictures of outings, strong men with fine moustaches, their caps straight for the visit of the photographer. One picture is of Ernest Jones, a relation, boy

89

sudden made a man in 1913, old by 1920. I have worked out that Ernest is great uncle to Allen Jones, uncle to his father. He sees the picture and have stood, too excitable. A little tea is spilled into his saucer.

'I have seen this picture somewhere,' he have told me.

'Seven men,' say I. 'Well, four men and three boys. You know what it is?'

Allen does not know so I stand up.

'This boy is George Moore, here is his brother Evan James Moore, here is George Moore the father, and this is Ben David. This is Archibald Dean, here is Wilf Vizard, and here . . .'

'Ernest Jones?'

'It is,' says I. 'Seven men from the eighteen saved. Underground four hundred and thirty-seven more, dead all. On top, John Moggridge, his head blowed away, dead faster than a wink.'

'How?'

'The lift cage, three tons, she do come out like a cannonball on the second explosion and John Moggridge still looking in at the noise of the first.'

'At least it was quick.'

'Quicker than for the four hundred trapped,' I have said.

'Brave men,' says Allen Jones.

'Rats,' says I, 'trapped and put to sleep, those not burned or skinned.'

Allen Jones is not hearing me. He says, 'They are dressed smarter than I imagined, and cleaner.'

'Scratch!' says I. 'This is boys and men in their Whit Sunday best. This have been weeks later after they do start to convalesce at the Porthcawl Miner's Rest and made some recovery. But see, the eyes are dead, men and boys, they are empty.'

My words have bounced off though, Mister Allen Jones is inattentive water and my message a boy's skip-stone. I think again of impolite as he steps round the room.

'This?' says he.

'The men of the Bottanic District, their huts down by the pit-head. The wives waiting for news.'

'This?'

'Alfred Milton, Bessie's brother.'

'The younger man?'

'Ernest Jones, the boy from the pit.'

'This soldier, the child?'

'Look more carefully, man. This is your grand-father. See the letters on his epaulette, the cross on his arm?'

'A medic?'

'Royal Army Medical Corps. He was not a fighting man, but brave enough in his way. The child is your father's brother. They lived at 169.'

'And this, who is this?'

'The fine upstanding deacon of the English Cong, Mister Robert Jones, your grandfather who married my mother.'

'He is in bed.'

'You are university educated, I have no doubt now. His leg twice broke and to be broke again at the charity hospital. After, he was not the same.'

'They are all so wonderful,' says Allen Jones. 'A rich history. And the stories, what stories there must be! I must go up to the mine to see it for myself, and go up over the mountain and see the terraces glistening in the morning sun. These pictures, I can almost smell the men at the face!'

'If I do not sit down and rest,' says I to this, 'I may faint for I feel queer.'

'Are you all right, Mr Williams?' my visitor have asked me. 'Is it your emphysema?'

I have coughed a little for effect and I am happy that I have not been rude, though my visitor deserve it. I have lied. 'A little. It is passed.'

And Mr Allen Jones, like a wind on the mountain top, he is on to other things again, his voice pit-boy soprano and he is excited like a girl might be.

'I have read Gruffydd Evans, W. H. Davies and Elias Evans, and just this morning, in Cardiff, I bought Michael Lieven's *Senghennydd*. But to be here, Mister Williams, to taste the valley, see the good people . . .'

That is enough. I rise, a bit too quick for Mrs Jones. I am thinking.

'I will take you walking!' I have said as quickly. I have thought, 'For just one more minute of English blather and I will take a fit.'

'But Mister Williams, your chest . . .'

'You will have a car, then?'

'It is just outside.'

'There's fine for us both, then. I will get my cap.'

Mr Allen Jones has a shiny car, red I fancy and the seats are like chamois and pale. It is a Jaguar and I have thought that to be a writer pays well.

'Are you sure you are all right, William?'

William now, is it? 'I am fine, Mister Jones.'

He have hesitated and then he have started the car and the engine is less noise than a clock ticking; a bee hums somewhere in the ferns.

'Go down yur,' I have said, making my Welsh more Welsh, a parody is it, like the English took Park Hamlet, Aber Valley and called it 'Sengennith' and when that was not pretty enough for them, have Welshified it to 'Senghennydd', two *n*s, and two *d*s, to be the new Rhondda. Why for there was never any sense, for the valleys were ordinary and lovely before they came, and black and dead when they were gone.

'If you're sure you're all right?'

I am thinking that if Mister Allen Jones have a Welsh core it is well hid, but I have bit my cheek to try and made my voice flat and slack. 'I will take you to the pit now, Mr Jones. Down yur. It is a mile or so.'

The car is a luxury, no question and very smooth, and there is a button I do press and the windows make a whush as they slide down. It have been wet, valley's wet, long and cold and drizzling and the high street is sticky-black and the tyres feel it. We are near the valley's dead end.

'It looks sad, Mr Williams.'

'Sadder,' I have said. 'And sad upon sad, dirty sad.'

There is nowhere further we can travel.

'Turn here,' I have told Allen, 'here, the little school yard.'

'But the pit?'

'We are here.'

'Oh,' Allen have said and I am thinking, 'There is romantic, is it?'

'It looks like rain,' he now have said, but I am already from the car and walking to the bronze memorial. My chest is angry with me, but I must be out of the luxury and back with the boys. Then Allen is behind me and I am staring down. He sighs. It is raining now, I think fitting, and down in the playground I hear the children of the village squeal and hop-scotch under a shelter. I am reading, but silent. Allen is reading. He whispers ghosts.

93

'This memorial commemorates . . .'

I am thinking 'English guilt.'

'. . . the 439 men who died at Universal Colliery . . .'

I am thinking, 'Were killed.'

'14 October 1913, the 81 men who died in the earlier accident in 1901.'

'Not a house without grief,' I am saying. 'Fathers, sons, cousins, two thousand orphans and me without a brother.'

'I didn't . . .' Allen says, but I have already said my prayer and am going to the Jaguar car.

I have taken off my cap and am glad of the rain that runs on my face and when Allen speaks now, it is a little slower for he is thinking too. Then he have asked me can we drive up the mountain and look down on the houses for still he have said, he needs to feel for the village. And now the rain is falling stair rods and we are sombre.

There are the old half-grassed slag heaps and the place where the Western Welsh coach must swing round to go back down the valley, but in between there is a track, up past an old ventilation shaft, a small-holding and a timber yard. It is narrow, but a red Jaguar car will squeeze where coal carts went. I have explained this and shortly we are on the top of Aber Valley and the dead town is below, higgle-piggled terraces along the valley side, their slate roofs glistened and a rainbow far off.

Allen has stopped the car and he have switched off the engine. In his neck and shoulders there is a heaviness, a slackness, and then he steps out into the rain to look proper. He have closed the car door but then he turns to me and says, 'Oh, I am sorry, Mr Williams, excuse me. I did not think you would want —the rain is very heavy.'

I am pleased that he is polite, but I am not ready to say so.

But my mouth is sudden wicked to me and slips a smile on my face before I can stop him. Allen nods to me and goes back to look at our valley. I think of my father.

When we are back at 172, Allen is now quiet and when I have changed and he have brought in a suitcase and changed upstairs, he comes to me more slow now, to ask what I know, and what can I explain to him. He have asked about Ernest Jones and how he have survived the explosion and he have asked about his great-grandfather and what is a deacon. But now he is not bizz-buzz like a grasshopper but patient. I have asked him, has the memorial quieted you? and he have said, no, but perhaps the drive there, the old houses, and then the look down on the village in the rain. He have said how there is grey and black and no other colours.

'And the children,' he have said.

The rain have stopped and some sun is out and I have just thought to say would Allen walk with me to the Commercial Hotel? We might together have a pint or two and a pie rich with gravy. But then there is a rap at the door and surprised, I have made a face.

'Are you expecting someone, William?'

I am not. 'It is perhaps someone for the Cong. I have a key.'

But I am worried before I lift the latch. There have been delinquents to my door, always with excuses, but I have known of them as burglars and rotten. And I am right, for when the door have opened we have the boy Ryan Pugh, and the boy Clint Thomas, both left school and trouble.

I have been formal but my guard up.

'Any odd jobs?' Thomas have said. 'We are looking for work.' He is perhaps not yet eighteen but a terror already. Fists like hams he have, his head shaved off and cheap gold in his nose and his ear. He have looked past me and I am thinking he is looking to burgle me first chance.

'Boys! Boys!' I have said. 'My place is like a new sixpence and shiny as a virgin's eye. I cannot afford to pay for odd jobs, but if it is a pint you are needing, I will be in the Comm just now.'

Here the other boy, Pugh, has profaned himself and he have gived me a look sufficient to win him a good slap, were we equal old and I did not suffer with the dust. I have thought it anyway and the boy looks daggers before him and his crony have gone.

Allen Jones have stood at the parlour door. His face is full of worry so quick I have said. 'Shall we go now? I feel a thirst and we will talk more comfortable in the Hotel snug.'

Allen smiles. I have thought he wants to ask me about my callers. I pick up my cap and turn to go out. He nods and I have thought how quick he has learned. We leave into after-rain.

In the Commercial Hotel, Allen have asked for red wine and Mister Iestyn Griffiths have laughed though I know he do have sweet white wine for some ladies. We have Ansells Bitter and it is fine. Allen have said it is not unlike Budweiser and when I have asked what is Budweiser he smiles and shakes his head. It is now I catch his eye.

'You never married,' he have said.

'Nor you?' I have answered. 'I am ninety-six. Are you forty?'

Allen have told me he is thirty-eight and then he have said very soft, 'Mister Williams—'

'William,' I have offered and he have smiled.

'William, we, I—'

He have lost himself and I am thinking about my father, but he have tried again, 'William, your father—'

'Yes?' I have said.

'It has never been acknowledged, all these years.'

'There is the Chapel's reputation,' I have said. 'More important than the wish of some boy to be called son.'

'Then you know?' Allen have said.

'I know, and you know,' I have said firmly. 'I know we both know.'

Allen is holding out his hand. I look to his face and the eyes smile with the mouth and I am pleased. I take the hand, much firmer than I expected. Allen is grinning.

'But,' he have said, 'I am not sure what kind of relations we are.'

I have worked it out a hundred thousand times. 'I am like Kitty's brother, and your father's uncle. I am only half-related, a different mother, but I am all Robert, and his curse have lasted strong. Philanderer or disinterested is the Jones germ and I am no philanderer.'

'So you will be my half-great Uncle William?'

'That is close enough, though I have not been convinced that germs divide equal but leap about in packs.'

'I am pleased, then,' Allen says, as Welsh as me.

And I am pleased too, for to be acknowledged, no matter how old, is to be acknowledged. We have settled who we are and to be related is enough. We have found a meeting place of minds and we have shook hands, but it is trivia now, best made ordinary and Allen have known this, and asked, to change the subject, 'Those boys . . ?'

'Bad blood,' I have explained, 'but bad environment too, for neither father have found work and the boys know nothing except their wits, their quick fingers and no future.'

'They're thieves?'

'Surely,' I have said. 'There is so little for them in the valley.

They have so much time and there are people from Cardiff and Newport come up the valley and peddle chemicals, that make the boys happy, or so they have thought.'

Allen have seemed surprised. 'Here, William?'

'Here, of course. So they rob. Here we have families broken, husbands exiles for extra assistance money, boys with no hope, the dole insufficient and eager men from all parts ready to help them pass the time.'

'I can't imagine Senghennydd and drugs,' Allen have said.

'Then you imagine,' I have said. 'They have took our green valleys and first raped them, and left them to grow black and blacker. Then there have been the sliding scale wages, but always sliding down, then strikes and starvation and lower wages still, and babies dying, and then when the unions were strong enough, the she-devil Thatcher have come along to kill the pits with a pen-stroke, policemen on overtime, and then buy coal from Poland. The choirs are going, all but gone, the rugby is going, the red life-blood is going; and for those who are left, it is drugs and stealing or fear and staying indoors. I am glad I am so old.'

I have seen that Allen is sad to hear this. Then Allen have told me of his dreams and of his writing. He have made some fame and his little fortune, but always it have been his dream to come back to his roots and immortalise his Senghennydd. But then he have said he have become empty now and he have said there is a place in his house for me for the rest of my days. I have laughed and said that things have not got so bad as have been painted.

'No, William,' Allen have said, 'the colour is gone from the houses, the faces, even the sky.' Then he have said, 'A couple of druggies should not be able to frighten you.'

'But they do not frighten me, Allen,' I have explained.

'Just the same,' Allen have said. 'My place is open to you.'

And I have smiled and nodded that I am grateful. I have said, yes, my valley is cruelly killed, its children damned, its old men bitter, but I have had my wholesome life and a little fraying at the edges does not make a good suit a bad suit, just frayed. And I have said too, that I am lucky for I did not have too many Sundays to concern me. And we did finish our drinks in some peculiar peace, not satisfied, but understanding our lot.

THE QUARRY

*T*HIS IS HOW YOU *make your crossbow. A piece of three-by-two pine you got from a building site, cut it up. Make a crucifix, two nails at the centre, otherwise the cross-piece moves. You'll have to buy the thick rubber, but no problem. Climb over the wall at the back of Feraro's Chip Shop, steal a few pop bottles, take them back in the morning for the deposits.*

Nail the rubber along the cross-piece. Don't put the nail through the rubber. It'll split. Use a couple of nails each end, bang them in either side of the rubber, then smash them over the rubber till it squishes down. You have to do two nails, otherwise it can come out. That happened to Colin Hicks. It's why he's got a glass eye.

Now, on the rifle bit, the bit you point, put a clothes peg. That's how you hold the rubber when you pull it back. You can't just have a peg, though. It won't hold. You have to have loads of elastic bands to keep the peg shut. We've got hundreds. Billie, Jacko and me, we lifted them from Woolies ages ago. When the elastic bands are holding the peg shut it's harder to open the peg, but you get used to it.

The bolts have to be about six inches long. If they're too short they fly off anywhere. Much longer and they aren't so accurate, I don't know why. There's plenty of arrow wood around. Make an end pointy, and at the other end cut a cross so you can slip the flights in. Use cardboard. You can make neat flights with cardboard and you can carry your spares in a baccy tin.

The crossbows we made could fire their bolts more than 200 yards. The record distance, the bow aimed for maximum flight and not accuracy, was more than five hundred yards, over the roofs of the houses opposite, over the dingle, over the dump, and into the spongy grass of the golf links beyond.

Practice a bit over the Gollers, hitting cans and shooting at the rabbits. You'll have to be a dead-eye dick. You won't get two shots.

You use your sister, practice in the front room. You tell Maddie it's the only way. You have to get good because otherwise, well just, otherwise . . .

She says, but if you get it wrong I'll be shot-in-the-back. She says it really fast, gasping, like someone on television, like one of the Swiss soldiers in William Tell, talking to Lamburger Gessler.

But you put pillows on her, on her head, her delicate neck, around her back, then tie them with string. Then you get her to stand in the doorway, face away. You put two baby's play blocks on her head, one on top of the other, but she moves. They fall off.

'Stand still!' you shout. You sound like your father. She flinches.

The second time she stands rock-steady. Frozen.

You've hung a curtain in the doorway, to catch the bolts when you miss. You aim high, thinking you'll work your way down, get good at shooting, but the first shot goes straight through the blanket into the hall and thuds into hanging coats.

'Wow!' Indoors, the power of the bow staggers you. You begin to think you really can fight back. Maddie has moved and the blocks are on the floor. You feel good though. You tell her, Maddie it's going to work. You pick up the blocks, put them on Maddie's head, step back, and load a second bolt.

'OK?'

Maddie says OK, but it's a long and drawn out OK, almost a sentence, questions.

FLACK!

Second shot you hit the plastic block, and splatt, bolt and block fly through the air. Maddie has lowered her head. She picks up the block and bolt. 'Cor Blimey!' she says. Then she says, 'Do it again!'

You shoot another ten times. You hit the blocks six times, twice you're too high, once you slam into the pillows, and once the bolt comes out all wrong, sideways, and *flangs!* into a cop-per BLESS THIS HOUSE above the fireplace.

You and Maddie are kids. You're tough but you're not stupid. You need to be tougher, bigger, and having a weapon helps. That afternoon, no girls, you, Billie, Colin Glasseye and Joseph Healey, you go as a gang on the five mile march to The Quarry looking for the Dirty Old Man.

All of you have crossbows.

The quarry is red mud, fine, shellac-like stone slivers. When dry, the banks of shale are soft as talc and the bravest boys know how to jump off the edge and tumble, half-run through the falling colours.

At the bottom is a deep black pool. They have all seen the surface break suddenly. They've told each other they've seen bubbles, but whether there are unknown fish or monsters in the deep, they don't know.

In the buildings, creepy, drippy, metallic, the boys and the girls used to play (Maddie too, before she got too sad), breaking windows, clanging bits of metal, trying to make old motors work, building dens, playing hide and seek. Until.

Until that once, when the Dirty Old Man was there and they didn't know. They'd been larking about, then they'd gone inside to share some lemonade. The Dirty Old Man was crafty. He had hidden somewhere and waited for them, and when they'd sat down, he appeared in the only doorway, and shouted. 'Right, you bloody buggers!'

He was big, in an overcoat. He had a fat face and hadn't shaved for a while. His eyes were yellowy and the eyelids sort of flopped open showing some of the red insides. He had filthy hands and filthy nails that showed through his gloves, the kind that have no fingers.

'Nasty little sods! I'll 'ave yer! Come 'ere!'

You all freeze, but not forever. You're Gaer kids. You don't mess about. Billie pushes you left and you grab the nearest girl as he goes right followed by Joseph and some of the others. Colin Glasseye climbs up on some bricks, grabs one and shouts, 'Dirty Old Man! Come 'ere, I'll smash yer face in!'

You can't remember how the stampede works, but it does. You're all, seconds later, outside in the sunshine, panting, raising little fists towards the old man in the doorway. It's another minute before you're aware Maddie is still inside.

It's you who realizes first. Something changes. You don't even think to enlist your friends. You run straight towards the old, too-big man, stop maybe six feet away, grab a piece of wood. 'Dirty Old Man! Let my sister out! Dirty fucker!'

He's leaning slightly, so big he fills the doorway. Now you see he's dopey. He has a squat bottle with purple liquid in it. Even from where you stand, you can smell it. Then behind, in the dark, you see Maddie's pale face. The other boys come up behind, shouting, tentatively braver. This is when the man steps sideways, turns and, like a gentleman to a lady, waves Maddie out.

103

Maddie comes forward, trying to be smaller. To get through the door she has to go within inches of the old man. He waves again, kindly. She shrinks as she passes, and then, just as she is about to reach the light, he grabs her by one wrist, envelopes her, lifts her up to show his power, roaring with some kind of sick mastery. Now she is upside down, her knickers showing. He smacks her arse, laughs, then puts her to the floor where she scurries away.

You all run, perhaps fifty yards, before realizing that somehow you lost the battle. You should go back, but you're not sure for what. By the time you've walked most of the way home the story is that a horrible old man captured you all and tried to do something to some of the girls.

You're going to get him. One day.

And this is the day. All the way you've been talking about getting the Dirty Old Man, and every now and then one of the boys points his crossbow at a tree and goes, 'Peeeow!!'

When you get to the quarry, you fan out into the buildings, backs to walls like film-soldiers then scurrying across open ground, rolling behind rusty iron, low walls. The drama fills you up.

You close in on the place where soft smoke rises, waving to each other, hissing, moving forward like Audie Murphy, Alan Ladd.

And then you're there, cats, commandos, and across a few feet of redbrick yard is his HQ. You were voted so you get up and walk out.

'Hey Mister!' and when there is no reply, 'Hey Mister!' again.

There is no movement, just the flabby light grey smoke.

'Hey Mister! I want to talk to you. You touched my sister!'

But nothing.

It's five minutes before the boys decide to go in. You'll go together and shoot him, shoot the Dirty Old Man dead then chuck him in the black pool.

Together, crossbows ready, the four of you stride towards the doorway. In your memory, this image is perfect, except it has to be the view from inside the building, for you see yourself like astronauts, the Right Stuff, striding towards the camera, heroic, determined, trained.

And finally, you are inside. You see the Dirty Old Man, half sitting, half lying, a smile on his face. His eyes are open, but he's not seeing you.

You close on him. All of you are shouting, Bugger! Fucker! Dirty Old Man! You stop perhaps six feet from him. He doesn't move, doesn't blink.

'Get him!' you say and you all fire.

Four bolts thud into him, into the thick coat, dull, hopeless, dropping to the floor. The other three boys turn and run almost as they shoot, but you don't. You reload, step closer, take careful aim at the face, and fire.

The bolt flashes into skin, the old man's grey cheek, deep and peculiar like into cheese. You stare at the man. He stares back. There is no blood, just a minute slick of something watery and brown on his cheek. You cannot get over how far in the bolt has gone. You reload, go forward again, still not convinced, and from four feet you fire at the forehead.

The arrow breaks skin but bounces off bone, but then, as if the old man is playing with you, he slowly lies down on the floor, on the unshot cheek, the arrow flights protruding from the other side of his face.

You crouch down, stare at a dead man. You poke him. Nothing happens. He's no different to a dead cat or dog, and this you can't get over.

You find the five crossbow bolts, then you turn to try and retrieve the sixth, but it's stuck firm in the old man's face. You need the others to hold him while you pull. You shout. Billie and Joseph come. Between them, they hold the dirty head down using their forearms. You work the bolt free.

Between the four of you, you agree to tell the girls the Dirty Old Man ran away. You leave him there. You never hear anything about him.

But, then, one night, Maddie is crying again, that special sad. Father goes out, slamming the door. You tell her the truth.

You say, 'See, Maddie?' and you tell her you are getting bigger, stronger. You can protect your sister now. It will stop. She sniffles and nods. Soon, you tell her, but we have to get it right, do it when he's drunk, when he's asleep. The first shot has to be good, might not get a second.

Soon, Maddie, promise.

POSTCARDS FROM
BALLOON LAND

*T*HERE ARE THINGS WE *should say, things we should not. And there are things we want to say but have never learned how.*

Dear Dawn.

We're in Disney Land! Dad promised us that if it was the last thing he ever did we were going to go to America and go to Florida and go to Orlando and go to Disney and stop in the Contemporary Resort. It's very hot. The grass is funny. There are hundreds of dead good things in the shops.

Love Rachel.

Hi Robert!

The Frog wants to go to the Magic Kingdom tomorrow and do all the girlie rides. Dad says we have to wait until Friday to go to EPCOT. The Contemporary Resort Hotel is brilliant! There's a monorail goes right through the building! It took nine hours to get here. We saw Concorde! Dad had a headache when we landed. Mam said it was because of the flight. Gotta go. Bet you wish you were here!

Love Ben.

Dear Millie,

I hope you and Dad are well. The flight was far better than I expected. There was so much for me to do that I forgot to be frightened! Peter was very tired, Rachel led him round everywhere by the hand. They bought me perfume. I told Peter off for spending but he just laughed and said, 'What's money?' The kids played Scrabble most of the flight. Peter fell asleep in my lap.

Your loving daughter, Margaret.

He was Peter. Soft red curly hair, blue, bright eyes, thirty-three; married to Margaret, father to Benjamin, to Rachel and to three-year-old Tobias. He read their postcards again. Rachel's card was a picture of Winnie the Pooh and Tigger in front of a blue-grey castle. The holiday was costing a fortune, but he knew he had never spent money more wisely. Before they left, he had told Margaret that this would be a once-in-a-lifetime trip and not to worry about the expense. It was all taken care of, he said. The look on the kids' faces when he told them was sheer joy.

Peter watched Toby pressing his face to a toy shop window in the hotel concourse. There was a time when he might have been impatient, but not now, not any more. Nothing mattered any more. He was on holiday. He wanted to wear a silly hat and look gormless.

Tonight he would make up another story for the kids and sit on that huge hotel bed with their spiky arms and legs hooked into him. He would whisper little messages to Margaret and later they would make love, very, very slowly, the kids a mangled heap on the other bed.

'Dad?'

He looked down at Rachel.

'Dad, can we have balloons? Like those?'

They were large, bright, helium-filled silver balls, stretching towards the sky on soft string. They bought three. Margaret tied them, one each, to small wrists. Immediately, Toby began to pick at his.

'Don't!' Margaret said, 'you'll lose it!'

'Free it, don't you mean?' Peter said softly.

She looked at him. He looked dreamy and lost.

They went for drinks, found a café. They were outside and a small bird appeared on their table, picking between their drinks, pecking at crumbs. 'It's pretty!' Rachel said.

Toby was the first to lose a balloon. He burst into tears. Margaret sat down and held him. Behind her, Rachel let her balloon go, looked up, then cried like her brother.

Peter pulled his girl into him. He felt giddy, but he swept her up and wrapped her in his comfort, strutting and spinning around, her gold head pressed into his hot neck.

'Hey, Sweetheart,' he said, the world still turning. 'There's a good brave girl. Fancy you knowing about Balloon Land.'

Rachel sniffed.

'I did, did'n' I? Tell you?'

She shook her head. Well, no wonder! They didn't know about Balloon Land! 'Didn't I ever tell you about Balloon Land?'

He called them together and they sat on the grass.

'I told you, Ben, yes? Last year?'

Ben shook his head.

'Well, I never!' Peter said. Then to the ground he said, 'They don't know about Balloon Land. Well I never!' He leaned back, his hands clasped behind his head, sun in his face. The kids were leaning forward. 'Well, I never!' he said and closed his eyes.

Toby squeaked at him, 'Tell, tell!'

'Tell us, Daddy,' Rachel said.

'Oh, Dad!' Ben said.

He opened one eye. 'I think you'd better,' Margaret said.

He sat up.

'When balloons are born, when they're born, they are flat and sad and don't know what to do. If people don't fill them up, blow them up, they never get to feel big or bouncy or pretty or anything.'

He had them.

'You know when you see balloons in their packets?'

Toby was nodding, his eyes wide.

'You know how flat they are . . . And they don't smell nice and they're all dusty?

'Well, they want to be blown up. That's what balloons are for.

'People were invented to let balloons be blown up.

'But there's a problem, there's a big problem when a balloon gets bigger . . .

'When a balloon is flat, nothing happens. They are just waiting there, waiting to be blown up. So they can do things. So they can go flying in the sky.

'People know balloons are very special things.

'That's why we have them at birthday parties and Christmas.

'People want to keep their balloons. They want to keep being happy. They think that if they keep their balloon it will stay a happy time and everyone will keep on having a lovely time. But!'

Toby nodded again.

'But balloons were made to fly. They want to go back to Balloon Land.

'You know at a party?

'You know at a party, how the balloons go up and stick on the ceiling?'

They were all nodding.

'Well, they are trying to go home.

'You see . . .' He pulled them to him, the warmth of his family an ache in his gut. 'You see, balloons are like very special birds. They can't sing, but they make people sing sometimes. So they come alive for birthdays, but then, after, they want to go.

'You know if you keep a balloon?

'If you keep a balloon, what happens? It goes all droopy and wrinkly and it gets sad. If you keep a balloon for a very long time, all its balloon-ness leaks out and it sort of goes to sleep again.'

Toby looked faintly worried.

'But if you let a balloon GO! If you let a balloon GO! It goes UP in the sky, straight off to Balloon Land. And if a balloon gets to Balloon Land it NEVER goes down and it's happy and bouncy and can fly for EVER. Balloon Land is full right up with every single balloon that you could ever imagine. Red ones, yellow ones, blue ones, fat ones, wiggly ones . . .

'So just think. Right now, in Balloon Land there's—'

'My balloon!' said Toby.

'And mine!' Rachel said.

Later, when Benjamin undid his bonds and released his balloon, they couldn't complain. Ben looked supremely satisfied. After lunch, Margaret bought three more balloons and diligently fixed them to three wrists. Just as diligently, the cords were loosened and the balloons released. Peter groaned, his eyes rolling, but the kids were already clamouring for more. Margaret thought it funny.

'Six dollars! How you gonna get out of that one, maestro?'

He was a little tired. He sat down and called them to him again. He need to explain, explain about balloon jams. 'Hey kids, come here!' he said.

'When balloons get to Balloon Land; if there are lots arriving at the same time, they have to wait outside. And they might go down while they are waiting. That's why we keep them on strings for a while. So we can let them go every now and then. To stop the jams.'

He looked to his wife, aching. Was that all right? Margaret smiled. She told them how, tomorrow, they could keep their balloons all day and then they could set them free, in the evening, after the balloon rush hour. She was still smiling, the sun coming through her hair, so Peter continued and told the kids that the jams were because Balloon Land only had one way in. The Balloon Land bosses wanted to make another way in, but balloons didn't know how to build entrances.

'So really, they could do with some grown-up humans to do the building for them. But it's very hard for humans to get back from Balloon Land, so they have to wait for volunteers.'

As they walked back towards the exits at the end of the day, a balloon sailed diagonally past and over them. Somewhere distant was a crying child, but their children were jubilant.

Margaret looked at Peter. 'You old sod!' she whispered. 'I love you!'

Peter was soundly asleep when they arrived back at the resort. Margaret woke him and he walked like a zombie into the hotel. The next morning she had trouble waking him, but he eventually stirred and followed her down to breakfast. The kids were asking about balloons so he said he would ring up and get a traffic report. He left them, used the phone and came back, nodding to Margaret, then telling the kids that Balloonway One was chock-a-block with balloons. Apparently, he said, there'd been a lot of parties in Australia the night before and they were still dealing with a back-log from the Olympics. They could probably manage a few balloons late that afternoon.

They stayed another week, used the jacuzzi every morning, lazily swam in the hotel pool as the evenings drew in. Then their fortnight suddenly was over and Nanna and Grancha Bill were coming to Orlando to take the children back to Grancha's farm. When they met, the two women embraced. Bill shook Peter's hand before pulling him close and hugging him silently.

The grandparents and the children flew back the following night. Peter tried hard to keep the mood light as they prepared to board their 747. Earlier, they had let five balloons off to a count of one-two-three and cheered as they sailed into space. Margaret had chosen to dress them all in Mickey Mouse clothing and little Toby was complete with a black big-eared cap. When it was actually time to go, they hugged, first as a family, then Peter alone held each child in turn, smelling them, feeling the breaths, sensing their heartbeats. After holding Benjamin, he stood back and held his hand seriously, like a man. He made a face at them all as their Nanna led them away.

Margaret drove the car south to Miami while Peter slept. They had booked into a wonderful hotel at the head of the Keys and the following day they walked hand-in-hand on quiet printless sand. They were caught in a sudden fat rainstorm, but chose to enjoy it, laughing, their heads back, savouring its warmth.

They drove on that afternoon, drifting towards Key West. They stopped at a little harbour where Margaret ate from an incredible seafood buffet. Peter had no appetite, but they sipped wine together and talked quietly. That night, they were asleep at six, Peter cradled in her neck, her gentle hands stroking his head. The next day they did nothing but lay together on top of the sheets, a copper fan phudding above them.

At their destination, they ate in romantic restaurants and drank in rough bars. In the evenings, they drifted along to the pier to watch the sunset. They stopped to buy books. Peter chose three, stopped, then replaced two. Every night she held him. They were closer than they'd ever been.

He had made all sorts of arrangements, all sorts of plans. Once he had had so many dreams. On their last day in the Keys, he had found a watercolour of balloons over Paris for Margaret, and from a staggered shopkeeper he bought a complete supply of postcards, all of balloons. While Margaret drove north, Peter wrote carefully on card after card. Each message was different, each card dated oddly. As they arrived back on the mainland, he was tired and his writing was less fluid. They stopped in Miami. Peter was asleep again, so Margaret arranged the check-in.

They flew to the clinic next day. While their plane drifted in to land, he explained again how she should use the cards. The children would receive one every birthday, one at Christmas, one on the day their father was born. He told her that Ben, Rachel and Toby should stay children as long as possible. He was going away, but they would know how to contact him.

Someone had to help build the new entrance at the other end of Balloonway One. If he volunteered, they could send him messages any time they wanted. He had arranged to be at check-in the first Friday of every month.

They could write to him, care of Balloon Land.

TOMATOES, FLAMINGOS, LEMMINGS

I ALWAYS THINK, YOU know, that working behind a bar is like being on stage. You have to look your best. You come in from the wings, all made up, and there's your audience, and straight away you're in the spotlight, you can't hide, and every night you have to perform, no matter what. You might have been short-changed on the maintenance again and the kids might need new shoes. Maybe it's your time of the month and you're feeling awful, but you have to do it, you do, look good for the punters. It's yer job.

I nearly went stripping once, after I was left in the lurch with my little Davey, but at the last minute, I bottled out. I think I thought that being behind a bar would be easier. I must have been mad. I've been here now for two years, one month, a week and a half; five quid an hour, tips, and a conveyor belt of blokes. I think I should've gone stripping.

All the lights, you know, and being on display, I suppose it's one kind of glamorous, especially early on in the evening, when the smoke's not too bad and the blokes are still close to being reasonable. When you first come on duty, you can't smell the beer or the fag ash. The cleaners do the place through with some special stuff that's got a really strong perfume and they brass up the taps really well, polish the mirrors and the bar top.

When you come on, it's nice and for a while you feel really great.

The blokes that come in the pub early, they're either the older fellahs, or guys having a quick pint on their way home from work. The old chaps, they're softer; they'll use my name and smile. Sometimes they'll call me luv, but it's in a nice sort of way.

'My usual, Gaynor,' they'll say, or 'Half a Mack's, luv,' or, 'Hello, Gaynor,' they'll say, 'How's the best-looking girl in Merthyr?'

Later on, around eight o'clock to half-past, you get the serious drinkers coming in; the lechers and the young lads who drink too fast, like they want to hurt themselves. I think they're the worst, the lads, and they talk like rapists. There's something cold and nasty in their eyes, even if it is only the drink talking. Sometimes they say the most horrible, the dirtiest things and sometimes it hurts. If it gets really out of hand, the landlord will say something, but most of the time we're expected to cope. 'Call it water off a duck's back and just keep serving,' Bill says. So that's what we do.

Every now and then you get a chance to say something funny, but you have to be so careful nowadays. These young blokes, they've got no honour. They'd hit an old man, two or three to one without a thought, so what's another barmaid to them? As far as they're concerned, we're all slags, good for only one thing. They haven't got a clue. I know it's the drink talking, but they still haven't got a clue. I wonder sometimes if they've got mothers. I just don't know . . .

You get chatted up all the time, of course. That's just the way it is. A nice bloke does it, maybe I'll go out with him, but only if I've laid down the law first. I've had marriage—and sex, well I can take it or leave it. I tell them, before we go out, but they never believe me. They believe me when I say goodnight on the doorstep though, just like I said I would. Girls should have the choice, right?

Blokes aren't very original. I think they get their chat-up lines off the back of match boxes or something, so when this bloke came in one night, not a regular, asked for a 6X and then looked at me and said there was magic in my face, light in my eyes, I was a bit taken back, you know, like you would be. I wasn't even sure I'd heard him right.

'You what?' I said.

He smiled a crooked smile at me. It was a nice smile. 'I said you've got a nice face.'

'Tell me something I don't know,' I said.

'Tomatoes,' he said, quick as a flash. 'People used to think they were poisonous.'

'What?' I said.

'People thought you couldn't eat tomatoes. They thought they were poisonous.'

It was fairly quiet so I said, 'I knew that.'

'Knew what?'

'Tomatoes,' I said. 'Poisonous.'

'But they're not,' he said.

'Some of 'em might be.'

'My name's Frank,' he said.

He left the bar then, finished his pint at a table, and went. I didn't see him for days. That night, after cashing up and wiping down, I had a brandy with Bill. I wanted to ask him if he knew this Frank, but in the end I didn't. I kept thinking about him, but I couldn't picture his face, except that it was pale and he looked like he needed looking after. I didn't sleep all that well.

In the morning, my flatmate Mary did us both a fry-up. She asked me if I wanted tomatoes.

'No thanks,' I said. 'Did you know they used to think they were poisonous?'

'Who did?' Mary said.

'Did what?' I said.

'Thought tomatoes were poisonous?'

I should have asked Frank that, but it never occurred to me.

'Everyone,' I said.

'Bollocks!' she said.

Mary had a way with words.

Frank came into the pub again about two weeks later. He was wearing light-blue jeans, a donkey jacket and that slightly off-centred smile.

I kept it cool. I said, 'Pint?'

He said, 'There are more plastic flamingos in the world than real ones.'

'Fascinating,' I said.

'Fancy trying the other side of the bar some time?' he said.

'No,' I said.

'OK,' he said. 'I'll have a 6-X.'

Later, when I told Mary (about the flamingos), she said, 'Who says?'

I wasn't going to get caught out again.

I told her, 'Me. I counted them.'

Just over a week before my thirty-seventh birthday, Frank came in again, a white-haired bimbo on his arm with licensed boobs. She was wearing bright red.

'6-X?' I said.

'Yes, please,' he said.

'And what about your mother?' I said.

I served 'em. They went away. I couldn't quite see them, but I heard him once or twice, laughing at something dirty, then her, hee-hawing like a ship's boiler that needed fixing. When he came back to the bar, I asked, 'Is your mother not well?'

He smiled. 'Did you know,' he said, 'that Lemmings are afraid of heights?'

I'd been practising. 'Yes,' I said. 'And did you know that in this country alone, an average of seventy-two people every day die playing bingo?'

'How many is that world-wide?' he said.

I was best part of thirty-eight years old next time I saw him, and my little Davey had been in Junior school a year. Frank came in with a thing about seventeen going on fifteen, plain brown hair, but the spit of her mother.

'Got time to talk?' he said.

'No,' I said, wiping down, 'too much to do.'

'Shame,' he said. 'I was rather hoping you might be ready to hop the bar.'

'Busy!' I said. 'You want a 6-X?'

'Please,' he said, 'and a Bacardi and coke for my niece.'

His niece? I couldn't help myself. 'Oh, p-ll-eease . . .' I said.

The little bird on his arm caught my drift. 'What d'you mean?' she said. 'This is my Uncle Frank, and you've met my mum already.'

Frank grinned. 'Did you know,' he said, 'that Oscar Wilde wanted to be a professional footballer?'

'What club?' I said.

'Why?' he said.

'Oh, I was just wondering,' I said, ''cos George Bernard Shaw once played centre half for Leyton Orient. They might have played each other.'

'Make the Bacardi a double,' he said.

I slept bad again that night. On the Saturday I went into town, bought the *Guinness Book of Records*, *The Daily Star Compendium of Little Known Facts*, *One Thousand Things to Say to an Alien*, *The X-Files Update*, and a second-hand *Whitakers Almanac*. My little Davey needed some new trainers and then we went to see *Pocahontas*. They made it look like a love story, but did you know that the real Princess Pocahontas was only twelve? I mean . . .

'Oh, yes,' Frank said that night. 'In fact, she wasn't quite twelve and her real name was Pooh-qua-hee-anthas, but John Smith couldn't pronounce it.'

'OK,' I said, 'What British team has the best win-lose-draw record in European competition?'

'Newport County,' he said. 'Played six, won two, drawn three, lost one. Goals for: twelve; goals against: three. Lost to Carl Zeiss Jena one-nil after drawing 2-2 away. You look lovely tonight.'

'Who scored the goals?' I said. He knew.

There are so many fascinating things you can find out, if you look. Did you know for instance that Ernest Hemingway re-wrote the ending of *A Farewell to Arms* thirty-seven times? I read a few of them. What if he'd given up on number twenty-nine? And did you know that no one wanted to buy that book *Peyton Place*? It sold millions! Britain's fattest ever man comes from Leicester, did you know that? So did Gary Lineker and Englebert Humperdink, and the first ever road traffic roundabout was built there, and Britain's biggest ever viaduct.

Corn Flakes are Britain's most popular breakfast cereal and even though banana trees grow as high as twenty feet, they're not really trees at all but giant herbs. And did you know that the longest banana split ever was over four miles long?

I bet Frank does.

One of the regulars asked me out. I was going to say no again, but I didn't. He's early fifties, but he says he's forty-three. I'd said no a few times and he was nice about it, so about the fourth time he asked I said all right, as long as he knew my rules. He's divorced and it still shows; he drinks a tad too much and he knows *nothing*. I asked him where Showaddywaddy came from (Leicester) and he didn't know. I asked him where the first roundabout was built. Didn't know. And as for the banana split, he just didn't believe that, but it's in the *Guinness Book of Records* and that is never wrong. I said goodnight on the doorstep, and thanks. He didn't even try it on for effect.

When I went to bed I thought of Frank, and flamingos. Frank told me once that in Miami there's a race track with thousands of pink flamingos. The track is dirt, not grass.

I know it's silly, but I felt slightly guilty going out with Jim. I should have stayed in and read up my World Cup statistics and a few more records. It's been a while since Frank's been in and I wanted to surprise him when he eventually turned up. But it's been ages and I have an odd feeling that he isn't too happy with me. Last time he was in he might have heard Jim ask me out, I can't remember.

I'm feeling sorry for myself, but I shouldn't. A robin will sit on a branch and slowly freeze to death, drop to the ground stone dead and never once feel sorry for itself. Life goes on, doesn't it? My little Davey is turning out fine, we manage, Mary is as good as gold, the job's sound and the boss is OK. What have I got to feel sorry for? Frank will come in when he's ready.

Two weeks ago I got some flowers. On the card it said: *He is too tired to sleep. Her face dances round him like sparks from a winter fire.*

I knew it couldn't be Jim.

The next night Frank came in. His smile was a little unsure.

He said, 'The longest ever banana split?' I told him, four point four nine miles.

Then he asked me, he said, 'Do you think you can fall in love in instalments?'

I gave him a pint and best part of a smile.

'Well?' he said.

I leaned forward. His eyes were blue. He pursed his lips.

'Ask me next time you're in,' I said.

I'm thirty-nine tomorrow. Frank's promised to come in. The plan is that next month we'll take Davey and Mary to Florida and Frank and me, we'll get away to Hialeah for a little honeymoon and to see the flamingos. People marry too young, and did you know that these days two in three marriages don't work out? Me and Frank, we're about to improve the statistics. Pint?

MEREDITH TOOP EVANS AND HIS BUTTY, ERNEST JONES

IN THE VILLAGES ALL down this valley, from Senghennydd down to Caerphilly, they call me Ernie the Egg.

I do not mind this, but for the record, I am *Ernest Jones*, poultry farmer, son of Robert Jones, Deacon, and they are my hens that run amok on the hill above the town. You may eat whosoever's pigs you wish, but it is my eggs that you shall have on your plate if you sup anywhere in the valley from Park Hamlet right through Abertridwr. My eggs is on the plates for most the best part of Caerphilly, too, though I know of some Cardiff eggs there.

Yes, I am rich, and the boys in the villages, and the old men, make jokes about me. Yes, Ernie the Egg I am, and with a few bob, and sought after by the Revenue, too, but I am wealthy by fortunate accidents and hard work, and with the help of God, and because of a great and ordinary man, Meredith Toop Evans, collier, and because I am shot in the neck in the Great War and because I am a failed scholar.

The hens have been my livelihood, but this have not always been so. Once I was to be a teacher, then a collier, then dead underground, then dead from a bullet in the Great War. That I am not any of these things is an odd thing for me, peculiar altogether, but facts is facts, which is why I will relate my story.

I was done with school two weeks short of my fourteenth

birthday, and I was timid, a bit too quiet. I had done an extra year because Robert Griffiths, teacher, had persuaded my dada I had a brain and could get a scholarship, but then, when I didn't win a scholarship after all, dada said, 'I am sorry, son, it is time now to earn your keep.' So I was late to go down.

Because I was late a collier, the other boys marked me down as different. They were already pit-hardened, with their broken finger nails and their coal-darkened scars, and they had that look already that the men got from working twelve hours a day in the dark. But me, I still noticed how black they got, and me, I was still afraid of that awful drop in the lift cage, the way you could feel the earth, and how you knew she smelt you were there, the way the darkness swelled. Too thinking I was, and cursed with it, and the boys knew it and played it up. Which was how it was I became buttied, that is *apprenticed*, to Meredith Toop Evans.

The first thing about Meredith Toop Evans was he was big, and no bones, I do mean bloody big. He was huge and slow, shoulders like a milk cart, fists as big as an apprentice's head, bigger than anyone I ever saw play in the pack for Wales, bigger than anyone I'd ever seen in all my fourteen years.

Toop was so big, it should have been a wonder he never played forward for Wales, but the other thing about Toop was that he was toop, I mean, that is, daft, only half-there, short of a pit prop or two. It was said that he was so toop he didn't even mind being called Toop and it was true that he had a slow way, in his body, and in his speech and in his head.

I remember once, when Ivor Price the Pontypool flanker was playing for Wales against England at the Arms Park and there was a loose ball fell at his feet like bread from Heaven. All Ivor had to do was pick it up and fall over the line, but the silly bugger passed it. We won the game, but after, Captain Dewi Thomas said, 'Fer Christ's sake, Ivor, why didn't you *think?*' and Ivor said, 'I'm big, I push. You can't push *and* think.'

Well, Meredith Toop Evans was like that, made to push, not to think, and when I started down the Universal, they made me his butty.

I had been set to start as butty to Mr Geraint Williams, but that first day, frightened enough to faint, I was in the lamp room when one of the boys said something cruel to me and I said something angry back. It was that or cry, and I made a face of it, but Toop saw what was really there and said to the foreman, 'Dai, give me Jones.'

Well, Geraint Williams didn't mind either way, so I was switched. Toop grunted, looked at me until I acknowledged him, and then lumbered towards the cage. I ran to put myself alongside him, like I was a pale tug under a huge, dark ship, and even in a place full of the odours of men, I could smell him, the damp grip of underground, strong tobacco, and over it all, the spearmint leaves he chewed.

I was not sure I should live, but I survived that terrible morning, hidden like a lamb in a hollow, in the lee of Toop's huge chest, my eyes closed, my teeth biting my tongue lest I might still cry, my stomach sensing the cage drop and my damn intelligence tormenting me, listening for signs of distress in the winding gear, the physics of the shaft. But I did not die of fear (as is obvious in me telling this, I know), and months later I was walking to the lamp room at the pit head to meet Toop. My dreams of being a teacher had faded and I had become a collier.

On the day of the 'Universal' disaster, that was October 14th,

1913, I started as I always did, at four-thirty. It was damp and dark in the huts, and we ate our bread and blackcurrant jam breakfast while the colliery officials were down for their two hour check, (mostly walking and little inspecting, but we all knew that). Then it was stamp to work and in our stalls by six. That was the way with piecework: you worked.

I must explain now, for this is a story told looking back, that some things that happened that morning were not as clear in the happening as they are now related. I know, for instance, for I have been told since, that the explosion was just before eight o'clock, and that it was smaller in its first occurrence than the 1901 disaster, and that an accumulation of coal dust in the tunnel ceilings sent death in fizzing jumps towards the levels where we lay dug, and loaded.

Duw, but it was terrible, terrible experience! Some men were crushed under roof falls, some shocked to a sorry quick death by the blast or burned bad by the fire racing along the miles of tunnels. And some were pepper-pocked by a storm of dust that flayed men's arms and faces, in a way so cruel, so cruel, they would have been better dead by flying tools or under one of the many falls.

Our district was the Bottanic and we were working the level the miners called Beck's Heading. As the blast roared through, the boys loading trucks were all blown down and tumbled in the wind, none of them breathing, not one ever to be a father. By rights I was another dead boy, but Toop had just called me under to help loose some coal. But for us under, by chance, and some of the colliers also under, there was only the sudden emptiness of air and a howl was all for us, like a wounded monster that rushed past us and away into the lampless dark.

I may have fainted, I do not know, but my next recollection was the close breath of spearmint and the voice of Toop calming me, telling me to be still.

I said, 'Toop, what has happened, Toop?' and he told me that there had been a terrific explosion and many were surely killed.

'And we must go out, boy, and walk.'

We crawled out from under. Even now there were thuds and bangs distant, and quick roars of air, like wild rushes of Hell. But then the air became still and we heard boys crying, and men groaning and it was hopeless, confusion, awful, and I was frightened almost dumb. But then I felt Toop's huge hand on my shoulder, and his rough, dirty fingers touching my face. He came close, so close I smelt his chew.

'We must walk,' he said. 'And we must not stop walking.'

'Yes, Toop,' I said.

'Give me your hand,' he said.

And I felt Toop turn his back, then my hand was on his shoulder, taken by his and laid on him like an epaulette, his hand still on mine for comfort, he understood me so well. Then he bade me be silent, and we waited.

Be deliberate quiet for ten seconds against your nature. It is a long time. Do much the same and wait for half a minute, wait longer. That is an eternity. After a while I thought I would burst from my fear.

'Toop?' I said.

'Shush, boy,' he said.

We waited, but the darkness, the faint crying, were too much and I spoke again. 'Toop?'

Toop did not speak, but I know he turned round. For I felt his fists, now open hands, take my head, my face to his, and I

127

felt his lips on my forehead, not a kiss, but as if Toop was breathing some of his hugeness into me. Very quiet he was. He said, 'Boy, be bigger now for we are suffocating, and there are men here who do not know what to do.'

Then he let me go and called out.

'I am Toop Evans, Newbridge,' he said, big and definite, like a lighthouse blows its horn to guide ships home. 'Shout out, one by one, your name, your stall and are you injured. Is David Thomas spared?'

Thomas answered. 'Yes, but not my buttee.'

'Will Morgan?'

Nothing.

'No? Alun Parry?'

'Yes.'

Like this, we found there were five men, Toop, and me. None bad, but all so tired we each felt like it was Sunday afternoon and a nap by the fire was the thing.

'Get up and walk!' Toop said, 'It is after-damp making you silly. If you sleep you will never wake up.'

'Monoxide?' I said half thinking, half-whispering, but Toop did not hear me. He was moving along the heading, punching men's legs, shouting into their faces. 'If you have wives, then get you up and walk!'

The seven of us began to walk, but the feelings in us were very strange. My head was in half-addled shape, but from my extra time with Mister Griffiths, teacher, and my Saturdays spent in the library down at Caerphilly, I knew that Toop meant we suffered bad there from carbon monoxide, a poison that kissed men to death, for it smelt of nothing, tasted of nothing, and first it seduced, made men soft, like perhaps they had drunk a little too much. The men wanted to sit down, for they were tired and stupid, but the after-damp was like this, a temptress, and to sit down was to die. Now Meredith Toop Evans, after twenty years of miners' jokes that he was slow to light up, was our intelligence.

'Walk,' he said, 'Or feel my fists!'

And the men walked, to sweeter air.

It might have been all, that as that, but we still had to get out. The men were now behind Toop, but we were still very tired and the after-damp whispered to each of us, 'Rest, just a minute, you will feel so much better.'

But Toop continued. 'Walk!' he insisted.

Later, I cannot know enough to be exact, but would guess the time to have been perhaps ten o'clock, about then, we came upon an opening, a crossing place for tram lines, some men and a boy. They were sitting. Their leader was a man called John Pugh, a hard, rough chap known for fighting in the village, and a foreman.

'John Pugh,' Toop said respectfully.

'*Mister* Evans.'

'We have walked, I calculate, best of a mile, Mister Pugh,' Toop said, 'from Beck's Heading along to here, where we have found you. We are looking for better air. The after-damp has gentled too many into a long sleep already.'

'The air is good here, Toop Evans, and safe enough. And here is where rescue is most likely. We should sit.'

'Mr Pugh,' Toop said slowly, 'Most respectfully, I do not think the air here is that good.'

'I am foreman,' Pugh said. 'And you are Meredith Toop Evans. I say sit.'

'The air is bad, Mister Pugh.'

'And thou art toop, Mister Toop.'

In the soft darkness, I felt Meredith pause and if there is a sound or a smell to great decisions, I sensed both.

'I will come closer, then John Pugh,' I heard said, very friendly, and then in answer, 'Come across, then,' from Pugh, and then a scuffle of coal dust, some shout or other, a heavy blow, more blows, and then Meredith speaking.

'Now, I am Toop Evans and the foreman is of an accident and resting. It is time to walk and any man disagrees, he can back his judgement against my fists. Get up now and follow my butty.'

Dai Pugh was not Toop Evans, but he was still a big man. He would be carried or die, but none were fit enough to do it. Then Toop spoke. 'Walk on, Ernest Jones!' and I heard him cough, then grunt as he shouldered up the foreman. 'Yes, sir, Mister Meredith!' I said.

At one minute to eight that morning, there had been four hundred and fifty-six men and boys underground and four hundred and thirty-eight were killed, one more dead above ground when the cage spat from the shaft and took his head as he was looking down at the sound.

Three hundred had survived the blast, but tall, short, clever or toop, one by one they went to sleep. But Toop Evans saved us and they gave him a medal. On it was written *Meredith Evans, Collier, for gallantry*, but I say it should have been for intelligence.

When John Pugh woke, we were sixteen of the eighteen spared and were in a pocket, sitting now, but breathing sweeter air, and more likely to be found. At first John Pugh was angry, but Toop whispered to the foreman and they came to an understanding, an arrangement about forgetting. But even this sweeter air was treacherous and when rescue came at last, all of us, even Toop, had given in to the sweet whisper of the monoxide and needed oxygen to return to life.

They brought us out two at a time, into rain, but I asked to stay with Toop and come out last, proud now to be his butty, and me, I thought, just a little bigger than I had been at breakfast. But it was into silence, not cheers for the numbers of certain dead was growing and hope for the rest not so high.

Truth is, after something like that, which only those who experience it can ever hope to understand, to be carried on a litter through the wives, the sweet rain falling, was to wonder at your own fingers and toes, to taste every drop of rain, and to feel and savour every breeze, the flapping of shawls, the crunch of boots in the wet gravel. And I was both terrible sad and terrible proud, almost in the pink, as if I was specially saved and saved because I was special.

Fifteen of us went to The Miners' Rest at Porthcawl, but not Meredith. He bade me take care of myself and to roll up my trousers if I paddled in the channel. He asked me would I ever go under the ground again and I said to hell first and at that he grinned, pushed his huge fist at me and walked away, his hands in his pockets and him whistling.

But then old Joe Kaiser started up and we were called to service. I was working in a bicycle shop in Fleur-de-Lys, but I went to sign up for the shilling as soon as I could. I was rejected. My lungs, they said, were bad. The after-damp, the accident, all that had made me unfit to serve the King. They had lots of volunteers, they said, but if I worked at my rehabilitation I could try again in three months. I was given a badge to show I was no coward and could drink in peace and was sent away.

It was the same later that year, the same again in 1915, in 1916 and 1917. But then, in the attrition, requirements fell, and in 1918, they took me on, fitted me out in khaki and sent me to France. And I was shot. So laugh at me boys, but I have been underground, and to France, and I was shot.

When a bullet goes by, it's like a buzz, something angry. I heard that buzz. I was with another lilywhite, a Borderer like me, and the bee-zing happened and Arthur went limp. I was too new to think and as I turned to him and bent down to help, I was shot too, no sound, this time, just my face hot, my neck strange and then, within a second I had voided and my legs gave up.

The bullet had missed my head and entered me at the collar, coming out somewhere lower, my backside, and now I could not use my legs. There was never any pain, and never any glory. I had been at the front two days and got a Blighty one. They sent me to Southampton on a stretcher, then on crutches, I came back to Porthcawl, then in 1919, with a walking stick, I went to Barry and they taught me how to keep chickens.

That's how I became Ernie the Egg and wealthy, but I have been under the ground and I have been shot for my country. I limp of course, money can't cure that, but I have a daughter and now a grandson, Meredith. I like to walk and I like the sweetness of the air on top of the mountain. I do not like the dark, but most times it cannot rain hard enough to disturb me. When it does, I wait in the lee of a mountain and rest, thinking myself toop for being out without a coat. And I wonder about Meredith Evans, collier, but he is gone.

HAPPY AS LARRY

L ARRY WAKES AT 03:50, takes a piss and, with his shoes in his hands, goes out through the glassed front door leaving the stale jam-and-cream sponge and the remains of Mary's stone cold tea. She had insisted, *insisted* on staying up to talk. Larry had taken to coercive or death-inducing mental incantations to make himself alone:

It's-time-to-go-to-bed-you-cow. It's-time-to-go-to-bed.
It's-time-to-go-to-bed-you-cow, so knock it on the head.

But Larry is away now, Larry is *en route* Larry is *dans le car*, *tout de suite* and he wants to get away *vitely*. He is leaving the Kremlin. It isn't even light yet, only the flabby yellow of two streetlamps, but the sodium glow's enough for padding Larry Peters to tread gently to the car, get in, lock the door, start up, reverse, and slink away. But as soon as he exits the cul-de-sac, once he is uncatchable, unshoutafterable, he puts his foot down. He flies.

In minutes, a country road, silver, dark birds lifting from hedgerows. Then another, better road, then the A303, and under a light, her, thumbing.

'Christ!' Larry says, leaning over to open the door. The girl is dressed in clothes all of the same colour except for one of those sixties-style Afghan coats. The all-over colour looks suspiciously like purple (shades of).

'Oh, cheers mate. It's cold out there.'

He puts the heater on. Doesn't even ask where she's headed. After five minutes he says he's trying to get to Stonehenge to watch the sun come up. 'Cool,' she says.

They are there. It's still dark. Larry wants to get out and walk. Mitch — well that's what her mates call her — says sure, she's warmed up now and it'll be getting warmer.

They are parked well away from the stones, and they duck over a fence and under the skyline, now banded with lightness (the birds are in full swing, even here on the bare moor). At first they don't see the individual shapes, more a sense of mass, but now, closer, lighter, they make them out. They are whispering, worried they'll be caught. Mitch has told Larry there's always security at the Henge these days but if they get inside the stone circle and sit down they'll be fine.

They scurry, more like naughty kids than criminals.

Now they are hidden, sitting. Larry is cross-legged hoping that the growing light will bring him something. What, he isn't sure.

'So, where are you going, mate?'

'Larry. It's Larry.'

'So, where?'

'Barnstaple, Bideford.'

'That it?'

'There's a sailing from the jetty at eleven. Lundy.'

'What's Lundy?'

She's getting louder. He whispers, 'Lundy Island. I just want to, you know.'

Light suddenly cracks open the sky.

'Know what?'

'I need some peace.'

'Oh,' Mitch says, disappointed.

Suddenly it isn't dark. Everything is grey. They are watching a water-colour form around them, but closest is the heaviest grey. The stones don't feel spiritual at all.

'That's it, then,' Mitch says, 'Back to the car!'

'I expected more.'

'Not the best time,' Mitch says, then she does a little bunny hop (she's been squatting) and looks at him. 'You were expecting a revelation or somethink?' He notices the *k* ending.

'Somethink, yeah.'

'Nah, mate, assall bollocks.'

So she pings upright, puts her hand down for Larry and pulls him up. They jog across the grass on their way back to the car. A Land-Rover pulls up, and a uniform steps out, but Larry and Mitch are over the fence, gone.

They stop at a Little Chef for breakfast. Larry wants to pay and Mitch gives him a look. He tells her it's just *breakfast*. They both have the big one and she orders extra hash-browns. It's been a couple of days. This is when Larry asks, so where are you headed and Mitch says fuck knows.

'I went there when I was twenty,' Larry says after a few seconds and Mitch does that look that is meant to be pretend, 'I didn't get the joke' and it's the pretending, stone-faced, that makes things funny.

In Barnstaple, Larry asks Mitch does she got a job, does she got a place she crashes, does she got—pause—a boyfriend? He absolutely *loves* swapping have for got.

'Nope, had a job but wanted to hitch around. Nope, had a

135

place but wasn't sending the rent. And nope, she doesn't do boyfriends. She gives him the look, a stare this time, but it's as serious as her 'didn't get the joke' stare.

He tells her it's just *fucking breakfast*. And a lift.

Just outside Bideford Larry is feeling an ache in his gut when Mitch says, so on this Lundy place, Larry, where do you stay? Larry tells her, there's a few cottages. He's rented a place called The Blue Bung, corrugated iron, guess what colour it's painted. He gets the look.

'How many does it sleep?' Mitch asks.

But Larry is going to be there a month. Is Mitch that dumb?

'I'm that dumb.'

'I'm not after . . .'

'That's why I want to come.'

'OK,' Larry says. He can stand her the boat money, the cabin is paid for, and who gives a toss about a few quid for food? They are in Bideford. They go to the Lundy Office.

The ship—is it a boat or a ship Mitch asks—is pretty damn basic and this time of year only half-a-dozen are going out. Twenty-four due back.

'Gets rough,' a seaman says, 'Carn always get the tender in.'

But today the river flows quietly, the estuary is flat, the sea barely rolling. They drink a lot of tea and coffee and Mitch goes to sleep on his lap and snores. He thinks she's pretending. Then they are at the island. He wakes her up.

'What?'

'We're there.'

They go out on deck. The island is a half-mile away and an

old rusty landing-craft is ploughing towards them out from a concrete jetty below cliffs. The crew are in blue overalls. Mitch has her nose pointed at the shore and her head is still.

'What's up?' Larry says and she tells him it's her thousand yard stare.

The swell is OK. The landing craft takes them, and they are ashore without getting wet. So, where is everything? Mitch asks someone and a few sweatered arms point upwards. 'Cheers!' she says and sets off dramatically, her first few steps childish raised-knee stamps then head-forward following the sweep of the only road up to the top. Larry follows and waits for her to slow down. She is young. He can pace himself.

The island is solid granite; earth clinging to it like mould. Sheep roam most parts, rabbits, wild horses. It has a castle, three lighthouses, a farm and the thing that Larry aches for which doesn't make him happy but lets him pretend he is not the opposite. The water they drink and bathe in is brown.

A tractor brings their luggage. Mitch is sitting on an iron grille step when Sam (thirtyish, dark, weathered face) chugs up, and dumps their gear. Larry watches Mitch watch Sam, who barely seems to see her before starting up and bruduggering away, bouncing slightly, with his trailer behind.

'Can I get a bath?' Mitch asks when he is out of sight.

'The shower's out back,' Larry says.

The weather's closing in. They play cribbage, then walk up to the Marisco Tavern. Mitch is edgy and Larry senses the problem.

'Here's a ton,' he says, 'You don't got to pay me back any time soon.' Then he laughs and says he'll have a pint of puffin, her shout.

They eat bar food, locally-caught scampi and fat, dark-brown chips; and they drink. Larry is steady, determined, measured, *aiming* at a specific oblivion, what he tells Mitch is slow-got drunk, heavy drunk that isn't drunk at all until you have to stand up to go home. Mitch follows, but a half to his one, except the first. She doesn't like the home-brew and starts on bottled stuff, Larry says is piss and air. Hey, she says, it's my money.

About ten, Sam comes in. He grunts to four or five people, grunts at Larry, then looks for an extra quarter-second at Mitch before giving her a special grunt and turning to the bar. Grunt, and his pint is there.

'Trouble with Sam is he talks too much,' Larry says.

'That his name, Sam?' says Mitch, trying to be casual.

'Lives here,' Larry explains. 'Been here eight-nine years now. Came the once on a day trip, decided he didn't want to go back.'

'He just stayed?'

'No. But he wrote to the manager and said he wanted a job.'

When Larry eventually stands, he does it slowly. He is not a drunk's drunk or an angry drunk, just this deliberate man who wants to sleep heavily. Mitch takes his arm and they pull together against the midnight wind, a lift of salt even this high above the sea, mixed with the soft smell of sheep. It's dark and they didn't bring a torch, so they walk back slowly, like stage drunks.

The island enjoys playing games. In the morning it looks like a bright July and the sun is sharp yellow, the air transparent, crisp. Lonely herring gulls droop in lazy circles out, round, and under the cliffs.

Mitch is refreshed and wants to go for a walk, so Larry says, OK, after breakfast they'll drift through the rhododendron tunnels on the eastern side as far as VC Quarry then climb to

Tibbets, maybe go to three-quarter-wall, even all the way to the North End Iron-Age forts and the wreck of the WWII bomber. He's showing off like a name-dropper and Mitch laughs at him.

'So you've been here before . . .'

The rhododendrons once threatened to overtake the island. They have to be hacked back every couple of years. But the walk up and down, in and out of the thick-stemmed bushes is delight-ful, breaking from scuffing tunnels to near-breathtaking bright-lit sudden view, cliffs, the silver blue water. The girl is enchanted and Larry feels peaceful.

He shows her the little pool so black it shines like cracked pitch, but when he tosses bread on the water something snaps at it suddenly, gobbles it under. Koi carp, he tells her, fat as a man's arm.

At VC quarry he tells Mitch about an islander, John Harman, who died in 1944 fighting the Japanese. The story is interesting enough — machine-gun nests, grenades, great bravery, death — but it's Larry's far-off look that Mitch catches. He looks like it is April 1944 and he's the Lance Corporal, dying from wounds philosophically, after having done his bit. She doesn't like the mood and asks if they can go home.

In the afternoon Larry snoozes and Mitch goes out. She wants to walk to the west side, sheep-spot, climb the church-tower, go up the lighthouse. Larry will come, but she says would he mind, she wants to feel lonely and wind-swept? Larry has his books, his diary.

That night they get drunk again, sleep again.

The next day is the North End, a solid walk, three miles over

139

exposed, weather-whipped granite track. They take sandwiches and bottled water. Larry wants to quietly sit and watch the wheeling birds so they wrap up well. When they get there, to a gully where Larry studied kittiwakes as a student, the place is bare, dripped with rain-rinsed bird shit. The clear grey cliff and abandoned nests look like a pillaged art gallery.

But Larry seems content. They climb down through thrift until they get to natural seats, God-left for spotty ornithologists. The other wall of the gully is less than thirty feet away. No, they don't fly off, Larry tells Mitch, they know they are untouchable, but right now the birds are in richer waters, all bar these odd, swoop-in, flail-back-out kittiwakes that look lost or as if they have misread travel instructions. When they call it sounds like a cry for help and Mitch thinks immediately of Larry.

On the Monday morning, Larry rises early. He makes tea, boils eggs, makes toast. He takes breakfast through to Mitch. She wakes with a grin and wide eyes and he says, 'Look, I'm going out.'

The wind is like a hammer and Mitch can hear rain hitting the roof so hard it's like a buzz-saw, a machine-gun. What for? She asks thinking this is a joke, yes? And Larry tells her it's Monday; he decided days ago, Monday he was going to the North End to watch for kittiwakes. And it's Monday.

'Have you *looked* outside, Larry?'

'Yes.'

She takes his chin in one hand, turns him slightly as if she's about to kiss him. Instead she looks him in the eyes, moving slightly as if she's trying to see round a corner. 'OK,' she says and lets him go. Larry pulls on his wet gear, leaves. When the door opens it's wrenched from his hands, slamming against the little house and he has to jump down into the garden and force it back against the gale. Mitch sits there, shaking her head. When the door is closed the sound is halved.

Larry gets back about noon, not that Mitch has a watch or there's a clock anywhere. She is playing Scrabble and when it's her other self's turn she gets up and runs round the table. Larry looks whipped, soaking, cold, older.

'Strip off,' she says, trying not to care too much. 'Grab a shower and I'll make a toddy.' But then Larry is so numb he can't undo things and she has to get up, throw a towel over his head and help him get undressed. She is as clinical as a nurse, and Larry is mere meat. His underwear is sodden and his private parts, when she finally pulls the pants away, are shrunk with cold.

She makes the shower cool and it still burns him.

After the shower, the place is like a steam bath in an igloo and the howling of the wind hasn't let up. They don't even want to make a dash for the pub. Larry is dressed in warm stuff, thin socks under fisherman's whites, but still he can't get warm. Mitch puts him to bed and climbs alongside him. She burrows in, hugging Larry close but stiff, wondering vaguely if he'll try anything, but Larry is inert, staring at the white wood ceiling. Once his teeth start and he bites down hard. But he doesn't stop staring. Mitch waits.

That evening is calm, there's even a late afternoon eggyolk sunset and wherever they look there is dark green calm. The sea is thicker, heavier. When they get to the pub, Sam is there, he nods to Larry and says, 'Ay-oy!' to Mitch. Later, when Mitch goes to the bar, he leans and whispers to her and she leans in, then away and laughs. Larry sees her coming alive. When she gets back to the table, Larry says thanks, then, 'I don't mind if—' and Mitch says, 'What, Sam? You're not serious are you?'

Larry is developing a cold and Mitch has decided she'll sleep with him tonight. She means 'sleep' but if sex happens, that's cool. Larry's hands ache from the cold that morning. He feels so desperately old, old and lost. This is the moment, unknowing, that Mitch tells Larry that it was nice when they cuddled together, snuggled together. They could do it again when they got back, if he—

Mitch is kinda neutral right now, she *likes* this guy, but whether it's the cold, or the ache, or the fug of cigarettes, Larry feels this is a sympathy thing and he lies and says he sleeps alone, always has, and in that moment, a life is determined. Mitch doesn't know it, Larry hasn't decided anything, but it was then, this second. The night rolls forward, Sam waits at the bar.

When they leave the Marisco, there's a fat moon rising late over the church. It's big enough to outnumber and outweigh the tiered, reaching granite and the church spire sits in its circle, captured. Had these two been lovers it was a moment they would have carried forever. Instead Mitch says, 'Wow lukkatdat!' and Larry tells her it's just an illusion, the moon isn't really that big.

In the morning, Larry does breakfast again. The eggs are soft and the toast cut into soldiers. For a second Mitch feels like she's eight and wants to cry. Larry is acting like a repentant husband, she thinks, while Larry just thinks this is a way to show how happy he is she's around, how grateful.

'We can do something,' he says, his tone, conciliatory. 'But I want to walk down to the harbour first. Say ten o'clock?'

'Sure,' Mitch says, but if Larry doesn't mind, maybe she could come down as well?

'Follow on,' he says, guessing that Mitch won't, and he pecks her forehead like a father does a daughter, gets up and exits.

Larry walks down the long cliff road, past two wooden cottages, a view of 'Brambles' and a distant shot of Millcombe House. The weather is squally, miserable, but he's wrapped up. When he gets to the water's edge, where it tries to creep up the slipway he crouches and tries to watch the same wave, where does it go, what happens to it. He counts waves, he guesses the height of the ripples, and it's only when Mitch's gloved hand touches his shoulder that he realises he is in inches of water and his hanging jacket is soaked.

'Not going for a swim, are we?' Mitch says awkwardly, and Larry says, no, not quite, but the waves, small like this, ripples, they fascinate him.

'Whatever,' she says, and he stands up, undoing his knees, but doesn't leave the water.

This is what happens next. They stand there. They get their feet wet. But Mitch isn't going to move, not if Larry doesn't. When the water is round their knees Larry looks down as if absent-minded and he's only just noticed all this water. Isn't Mitch cold, he asks, and she says of course she's fucking cold. So Larry turns and splodges out of the water, and Mitch turns after him and splodges out of the water, and Mitch, who doesn't fancy Larry, hardly at all, *desperately* wants to go back to the Blue Bung and make love to him, and Larry, who aches to be wanted, to be held just once more, but is terrified of sympathy, desperately wants to go back to the Blue Bung and make love to Mitch, but all they manage is to wrap tightly into each other and squelch upwards, up the hill, into the wind, away from the sea.

They get back to their warm, warm Blue Bung, but somewhere their independent secrets have turned to humour. It isn't too late, all Mitch has to do is take a playful swipe at Larry, he'll duck, grab, and it will happen. All Larry has to do is throw a towel at Mitch and she'll throw it back and they'll end up in bed (the sex will be good) and Larry will live, Mitch won't be sad. But they don't. They are friends. They have a nice, slow day. They have one pint in the tavern at lunchtime, they play a game of Monopoly in the afternoon and Mitch cheats blatantly. When Mitch showers, Larry finally finishes Bleak House, one of his promises, then they go back to the pub.

They eat a fantastic turbot, white flesh, brilliant, taken that afternoon. They drink, they talk. At the bar, Mitch laughs with Sam and he puts his arm round her and Larry smiles. It's about ten. Larry finishes another book and puts it down (*Being There*, Jerzy Kosinski). Mitch doesn't see him go out to the toilet.

Mitch doesn't see Larry go out to the toilet. (Sam is whispering, something.) She doesn't see Larry walk past the moonlit church, their little, warm Blue Bung. She was laughing then. She doesn't see Larry, calm, peaceful, walk down to the harbour, but she sees his book on the table next to his half-drunk pint. She doesn't see Larry unchain the rowing boat, doesn't see him push off, doesn't see him bang into the waves coming out of the bay.

Mitch tells Sam, 'Leave it out!' She doesn't know where Larry's got to. Can someone see if Larry is in the gents? As Larry strokes away from the shore, someone comes in and says, Larry's not out there. Mitch picks up the little book and leaves. Larry isn't in their Blue Bung, but there are things on the table, an envelope, Larry's wallet.

Mitch runs out, falls down the step, gets up, runs down the cliff road. But it's dark, the moon is not quite up and apart from the silver of breakers she can see nothing. Larry, not far out, has stopped rowing.

There's moon, half cloud-rubbed, half cliff-hidden, but there is light. Mitch looks out to sea, out to see, but there is nothing there. Larry is silver, same as a wave, and as they look at each other, both blind, the moon rising, the wind dropping, both of them wonder.

But Larry is smiling, happy as Larry as he rolls, slowly, over the side.

ACKNOWLEDGEMENTS

The author would like to thank the judges and editors of the folllowing prizes and publications where stories from this book first appeared:

'Ballistics' was first prize winner of Lichfield Short Story Prize and was first published in print in *Whispers & Shouts*, Ireland; 'Miguel Who Cuts Down Trees' was first prize winner and first published in *Cadenza;* 'The Smell of Almond Polish' won first prize and was first published in *Focus on Fiction*; 'Mother, Questions' was joint first prize winner and first published in *Buzzwords*; 'Green Glass' was first prize winner and first published in *Buzzwords*; 'L for Laura; L for Love' was first prize winner of Southport Short Story Prize; 'An Old Man Watching Football After Sunday Lunch' was first prize winner of Pencil Short Story Competition, Bantry, Ireland; 'The Fucking Point Two' was first prize winner Lichfield Short Story Prize; 'Obelisk' was first prize winner and first published in *Connections*; 'Spectacles, Testicles, Wallet & Watch' was first prize winner and first published in *Peninsular Magazine*; 'The Last Love Letter of Berwyn Price' won second place and first published in The Bridport Prize Anthology; 'The Bastard William Williams' won Second Place and first published in The Bridport Prize Anthology; 'The Quarry' was first prize winner, Momoya, and published in the *Momaya Anthology*, London; 'Postcards From Balloon Land' was second prize winner and first published in *Raconteur;* 'Tomatoes, Flamingos, Lemmings' was Editor's Choice, Fish Prize and first published in *Dog Days (Anthology)* Fish Publishing; 'Meredith Toop Evans' (a shortened version) was runner up in the Rhys Davies Memorial Award. The longer version here was first published by Atlantic Monthly Magazine, in *Atlantic Monthly Unbound.*